Walking

with Albert

and Other Stories

Walking

with Albert

and Other Stories

by
Keith Weaver

IGUANA

Copyright © 2019 Keith Weaver
Published by Iguana Books
720 Bathurst Street, Suite 303
Toronto, ON M5S 2R4

Editor: Paula Chiarcos
Front design: Daniella Postavsky

ISBN 978-1-77180-331-1 (paperback)
ISBN 978-1-77180-332-8 (epub)
ISBN 978-1-77180-333-5 (Kindle)

This is an original print edition of *Walking with Albert*.

Table of Contents

Somewhere in the Middle

He was pretty sure it was July, though he had no idea what day or date it might be. But that wasn't important. The sun had just risen, it was a fine day, there was no wind, and Archie was content to examine the holes in his socks and underwear as he sat in shallow water at the beach washing them. A much bigger problem concerned him: the broken wheel on his shopping cart. But when he thought about it, Archie realized that, at the moment, he was more than just content. He was in one of those brief happy periods, when external events and internal demands were still and silent. He was not starving and he knew how to deal with low-level chronic hunger. He was not in any pain, and his body had long since got used to sleeping on hard or irregular surfaces and having his sleep interrupted.

He was not in discomfort. The air was warm. The water was cool, but not cold, and after the initial shock it felt good on his buttocks and genitals. He could take his time washing his socks and underwear. Two sticks pushed into the sand behind him would allow his underwear, his only pair, to dry in the morning sun, and this would take little time.

At this hour of the morning, there would be quite a few joggers out, but they were further inland, on the path and the boardwalk, making it easy for him and them to avoid each other. Here on the beach, there was rarely anybody out before the sun was well up in the sky, by which time he would be finished, dressed, and on his way again. And for this reason he was surprised, a little unsettled, but also a bit intrigued to see a figure walking slowly toward him. The figure was quite a distance away, so Archie couldn't see whether it was a man or a woman. If it was a woman, she would most likely move much further up the beach once she got close enough to see his situation and make her way past him quickly to avoid any embarrassment to either of them.

In a few minutes, Archie had finished washing his underwear, and he draped it over the two sticks. His cotton shorts looked forlorn in their grey holeyness, but the inevitable skid marks resulting from his poor and erratic diet were gone, and the garment smelled at least neutral if not fresh. The figure on the beach was now a hundred metres closer, from the gait it looked like a man, and he seemed either to be reading something or looking at one of those telephone things everybody carried now. Archie turned to the task of washing his socks, and thinking idly about the day ahead. It was a standard routine that he followed, a series of end-to-end events that stretched through the day, requiring no thought and avoiding any occasion for it. His was a small world, but small worlds are easier to manage. His socks were also grey but were now rid of that acrid odour they always developed after three or four days and nights of continuous wearing. In a few minutes, when the sun had done its work on his underwear, he would dry himself on the fragment of beach towel he had found in the spring, a piece of terrycloth that now was also on the verge of expiring, then he would dress and take his socks to the canoe club where he would lay them on the heavy black plastic that covered the upturned canoes on the beach next to the club house. There, his socks would steam-dry in no time under the morning sun.

But this would not happen, he realized, before the strolling figure reached him. The figure was now less than a hundred metres away; it was a man, youngish, and he stopped, his book still held up at reading level, and was looking out onto the lake.

"To hell with it", Archie said. He rose from the water, walked naked to where his ragged towel was lying on the already warm sand, and began drying himself. Having finished that, he walked back to his underwear, now waving lightly in the first breeze of the morning, and bent to feel how dry it was. Still quite wet. He walked toward the canoe club, spread out his two socks and his underwear on the black plastic, which by now was very warm, and sat down on a nearby canoe. In less than three minutes, his underwear was sufficiently dry; he pulled it on, then his trousers and shirt, and sat waiting for his socks.

The man continued to make his way along the beach, not deviating to avoid him. *Shit.* Archie tried to focus on his socks, now steaming nicely, but he had the image of the stroller before him: clean shaven, short black hair, good jeans, expensive-looking tan leather shoes, white cotton shirt decorated by fine dark-blue stripes, grey windbreaker, obviously not cheap. The figure stopped again to look out at the lake, but after a couple of minutes he turned and began walking toward Archie. *Shit!* But Archie made no move apart from taking elaborate care with his socks, turning them inside out and placing them again on the black plastic.

The man stopped about ten feet from Archie. "Good morning." After no response from Archie, the man said, "Beautiful morning. This is the first time I've walked along here this time of day. Didn't realize how pleasant it is."

Archie just gave another turn to his socks, which were starting to look like miserable strips of salt cod.

"My name's Michael", the man said.

A slight nod from Archie.

Michael closed his book and slid it into a jacket pocket. "I was thinking of having a cup of coffee and some breakfast. Would you care to join me?"

This spoke directly to Archie's stomach, which, in an unauthorized unilateral action on behalf of the rest of his body, caused a flicker to cross Archie's face. Neither Archie nor Michael said anything for a few seconds.

"There's quite a good place just up the beach. I'd be pleased if you came along. I would be grateful for the company."

"I thought you said you didn't know this area", Archie said, his voice light, a bit hoarse and hesitant, as though he was out of practice in speech.

"No, I said this is the first time I've walked this beach this early in the day. But I've had late breakfast here, and it's good."

"I can't just leave my stuff here."

"Bring it with you."

"Can't. Wheel on the cart's broken." Archie indicated the shopping cart sitting next to a canoe and canted at an odd angle.

"I'll help. We can walk it along on two wheels."

"Naw. You go ahead on your own."

"I really would like the company. And I think you'd enjoy some breakfast. But it would all be a lot easier if I knew what to call you."

"Archie will do."

"Good. Let me help you, Archie."

Michael walked over to the cart, gave it a quick look, picked it up at the front end by its basket, and moved it back and forth. "Looks like it will move fine."

Archie shrugged, stepped behind the handle of the cart, and the two of them began rolling it along the path. The breakfast place was called Ollie's, and had a patio arrangement out front that held six picnic tables. Ollie opened at dawn, and his "restaurant" was really just a large kiosk, but he was known for his breakfast menu.

"Let's take a table right at the front, by the beach, so nobody will get between us and the morning", Michael said and angled the cart that way.

Archie moved along with him. They placed the cart next to the outermost table and both sat down on the same side, facing the sun, Ollie's large stand to their left and Ollie looking on in interest.

"What would you like, Archie?" Michael asked quietly.

"Coffee and a piece of toast will do fine, thanks", Archie replied without looking at Michael.

"You sure you wouldn't like a glass of orange juice, two eggs on your toast, and some bacon and mushrooms on the side? That's what I'm having. I'd be pleased if you joined me. On my quarter and no strings attached."

Archie flicked a glance at Michael, nodded vaguely, and then turned to look out over the lake again.

"Excellent! I'll be right back."

In less than three minutes, Michael returned carrying two large glasses of orange juice and two sturdy mugs of coffee on a tray. He set them down, retook his seat, picked up his orange juice, and said "Cheers!"

"Cheers", Archie said, almost under his breath.

They sat for a while and looked out at the lake. The sun had now climbed several diameters above the horizon, and it was warm on the face. Michael stripped off his jacket and sat in his short-sleeved shirt. Neither one said anything for a few minutes. A light breeze had arisen and small waves began lapping rather insistently at the shoreline, as if to make the point that they shouldn't have the sole responsibility for filling the conversational void.

"You come here often?" Archie asked, looking directly at Michael for the first time.

"Two, maybe three times a week, but like I said, not this early."

"Aren't you concerned about being seen sitting with a guy like me?"

Michael drained the last of his orange juice and took a first sip of coffee. "Ohhh! Hot!"

There was a short pause. "We're just two guys sitting having breakfast and chewing the fat", Michael said.

"Unlikely couple of guys." Archie sniffed and grunted dismissively.

Another sip of coffee.

"Yeah, Archie, we're different. But so what?"

"I don't do breakfast", Archie responded, not looking at Michael.

"Well, you can make today an exception."

"What about a shave? A haircut? Some clothes?"

"Those are just appearances. But let's be blunt, shall we? Yeah, we're different. You don't have a good set of clothes to your name, and the cost of what I'm wearing easily tops six hundred dollars. So what?"

Archie set down his half-full glass of orange juice. "I have to leave."

"You think I'm making fun of you, don't you? I'm not. I'm making fun of me."

"I'm not interested in riddles", Archie said rather coldly and made to rise from the table.

Michael placed a hand on his arm. "I'm sorry. I'm not doing a good job of this. Please stay. Let's drink our coffee and enjoy the sunshine. Our breakfast will be ready in just a few minutes. Then I'd like to tell you a bit about myself."

They each took another sip of coffee and resumed looking out at the lake. The breeze was warm and the scene was peaceful. Michael cast a surreptitious glance at Archie and saw Archie's very faint smile as he directed his deeply tanned and weathered face to the sun and squinted into the light dancing on the water.

He looks at least fifty, Michael thought, *but I'll bet he's only about thirty, not more than thirty-five.*

Just then, a bell sounded behind them. Michael smiled suddenly in anticipation. Archie turned to look at Ollie's kiosk. His face reflected uncertainty and some concern that events were well out of his control. "The breakfast gong", Michael announced. "I'll be right back." A minute later, they were both seated before large plates of eggs, toast, bacon, mushrooms, and sausages.

"Bon appétit!" Michael said.

Archie nodded and stretched out a hand to grab a piece of bacon, but then stopped, excused himself, rose from the table, and headed toward the kiosk. Three minutes later, he came back, sat, and picked up a large piece of bacon in fingers that were now clean.

They ate in silence for a while.

Without warning, Archie asked, "Why are you doing this?"

"Buying someone breakfast? It's not unheard of. Besides, I wanted to talk to you."

"You don't even know me."

"No, I don't. But I wanted to talk to an ordinary person."

"What's an ordinary person?" Archie asked gruffly. "I'm not ordinary. You're the one who's ordinary."

"I've just spent ten years at university, so, no, I'm not an ordinary person any longer. And by that, I don't mean I'm special. I mean I've been pumped full of unordinariness, been prepared for an unordinary world, so I've lost something."

They ate in silence a few minutes more.

"What did you study?" Archie asked.

"I spent six years studying English literature, then four years in law school."

"So, you're a lawyer?"

"I have a law degree, but I haven't yet taken the final step that will allow me to practise law."

"Are you going to do that — take that final step?"

"Probably", Michael said. "Otherwise, it wouldn't be a very good use of time. Although I'm no longer convinced that it was a good use of time anyway."

"But it would allow you to make a lot of money."

Michael finished eating, set down his knife and fork, and wiped his mouth and hands on his napkin.

"Now we get to the real heart of the matter, Archie. If I spend my time making a lot of money, what am I going to use that money for, supposing, of course, that I have any time left to use the money on anything?"

"Well", Archie began, "you could use some of it to buy more expensive jeans, shirts, shoes, jackets..." Archie looked out over the lake again. "That would be one thing distinguishing you from me."

"Distinguishing", Michael said. "It sounds to me as though you might have spent some time in university as well."

"One year."

"Why did you leave?"

"Don't remember."

"How did you get into your present way of life?"

"Just happened."

"Well, you know what? That's how I got into law school. It just happened. Now, four years later, I'm doing the thinking I should have done ten years ago."

"Still", Archie pursued, "you've got something — you have potential."

"But, potential to do what and for what purpose?"

Archie shook his head. "I don't see how talking to me will be the least help to you."

"No?" Michael raised an eyebrow. "I'm making some assumptions about you that might be all wrong, but I'm thinking that you're at another extreme. You probably take things one day at a time. You probably don't worry about anything too far in the future or about anything you can't change easily or quickly. At one level, your life is very simple, and you're able to spend a lot of it outside." Michael waved his arm indicating the lake, the sky, and the park behind them.

"You don't know anything about me", Archie responded somewhat truculently.

"You're right. I don't. I'm just guessing. But I think I'm not too far off."

"What does it matter to you anyway?" Archie shot back.

"It matters", Michael replied. "We're talking. I want to know something about the man I'm talking to. Am I about right?"

"What if you are?" Archie said, appearing to lose interest in the exchange.

"Just hear me out, please. Let me tell you one of the paths I could just fall into if I went ahead and used my law degree. I did very well in law school, so there would be expectations. I might try to meet them. I could end up worrying whether my BMW was getting too out of date, whether its colour was no longer 'in', whether I should move to a higher model number. I could worry that a three-thousand-dollar suit doesn't send quite the right signal, and that maybe I should move to a higher price range. Or maybe having five suits isn't enough — *Michael, didn't you wear that suit to the president's meeting just last week?* — maybe this, maybe that, maybe something else. And that's without even worrying about my work, my rate of advancement, and so on. I think one could call that an extreme without any exaggeration at all."

"So you go for morning walks on the beach looking for the answer?"

"No. I get outside at an unaccustomed time and look for inspiration."

"And did you find it? Or is it in that book you were reading?"

Michael reached over to his jacket, pulled out the book, and laid it on the table. "It does help me think."

Archie picked up the book and held it in one hand, as if weighing it for its wisdom content. "Epictetus, eh? What, then, is to be done? But Tolstoy taking all the credit."

"Ah, I guess you studied philosophy."

"I read a lot of stuff for one year. Not quite the same thing as *studying.*"

Archie didn't put the book down, but looked at the back cover, opened it at random, and spent a few minutes reading.

"How long ago was that?" Michael asked. "Ten years?"

Archie looked up sharply. "Twelve. But most people would put me at fifty or older."

After reading another minute, Archie closed the book. "So, what are you going to do? Presumably not sit on the horns of a dilemma."

"No, not sit on any horns. I need to find some useful middle course, somewhere between what an aspiring someone like me would set out to do and what someone like you does."

"Me?"

"Yes. Twenty-five hundred years ago, you might have been a philosopher, walking around thinking and discussing. Today you just walk and push a cart. Maybe I could run informal legal classes in the park. Or brush up on some philosophy and get into scholarly public disputations. The trouble is, neither of those would work today, in the sense that neither would let me be reasonably content and at the same time get enough to eat. Despite all that we know, despite all the new professions and occupations that never really existed in the past, the system has us well and truly snookered."

"The past. What's that?" Archie said, sounding like he was being drawn into the discussion reluctantly.

"Not a bad comment", Michael said. "In a real sense, it doesn't matter anyway. Today is all we've got."

Michael took another sip of coffee, keeping his eyes on Archie. There was a pause here.

"So, what do you think, Archie?"

"Doesn't matter", Archie said, shrugging. "I've dropped out. Don't do people."

"So, what are you saying?"

Archie just looked out over the lake. The silence, almost companionable, stretched out to three, four minutes.

"Where do you live, Michael?"

"Just down the beach. Moved there two months ago. Wanted to be someplace where I could hear nature, feel soothed, and I thought that waves on the beach would meet that need."

"And does it?"

"A bit too well. It was listening to the waves that got me into this train of thought." Michael looked at Archie. "Why did you want to know where I live?"

There was a long pause here. "Well ... I thought I might visit. See if I could borrow one or two of your books."

Michael gave Archie an odd, questioning look.

"I don't think I've spoken as much in the past two years as I have so far today. It's, well…"

They both looked out over the lake.

"Do you think we could get together again sometime for another chat?"

Michael turned to Archie and smiled. "More coffee?"

Blueberry Pie

At five forty-five, I had the road to myself. The east was a Saturday morning Nebuchadnezzar red, temperature rising, and my car seemed to be in as good a mood as I was, heading back to my hometown, just for the weekend — a trip long put off and only part of the reason for my light mood.

The other part was Clairaut. Clairaut had happened. Last evening. Seven thirty. The technical problem I had been butting my head against suddenly collapsed, and the Clairaut equation had appeared to me out of the rubble. Within half an hour, I had scribbled notes for the solution and had confirmed it by a worked example. I had my answer. Match over. Problem down for the count.

What had seemed earlier like just a welcome break, a temporary respite, now was a reward, an evening with former primary school friends. Six of us had agreed to meet. A reunion postposed far too long, for decades, in fact, and postponed for all the usual trivial reasons. I could picture the other five. As they were then, of course. Twenty-five years ago.

I was intrigued over what we might talk about, what they would ask me. It would be all general stuff, I supposed. And whatever they asked, my replies had to be low key, not anything that might seem threatening or overwhelming. None of this Clairaut stuff, for instance. They might think I was being just a show-off, a smart-ass, who was putting them down, and would have no idea what I was talking about, and I definitely didn't want that. Most of the things in my life didn't matter anyway in the context I was about to enter. The Clairaut problem was just a little personal victory, something I could celebrate privately. This would be their reunion more than mine, on what was their home ground but no longer mine, and it was the reunion itself that mattered. Chuck, Reg, Bobbie, Andy, and Wally. They had all remained locally. Only I had gone off to the bright lights. But just recalling the diminutives, those names from our untried, ingenuous youth, convinced me that beer and barbecued steak would put us all back on the same footing.

Through the slightly opened window, warm summer air puffed into the car. As the highway rose toward Orono, Lake Ontario glittered behind me in the sunshine. Somewhere within the deep pine forests that covered the moraines, tree spirits schemed and plotted. In due course, choirs of grasshoppers rasped from within their fields of oats and hay, and stands of maple drifted past.

Back then, that had meant bicycles, canoes, and snorkels in summer, and toboggans, hockey sticks, and skates in winter. In all seasons, we were an inseparable sixsome. Sharply etched memories of sensations returned. Blacktop road surface that scorched feet and made their owners dash for the next patch of shade. The tingly immersion in bubbles just after one jumped off the bridge into the river. The mixed feeling of loss and anticipation as one got ready for another school year. The golden anaesthesia of autumn, as everything slipped into its pre-winter sedation. The tang of wood smoke in the air. The first thin crust of ice on puddles.

A voice within me said that *The Great Lover* was passé and advised that I drop the Rupert Brooke bit.

I was passing the old Wilson place, perched up on the hill to the left, still sitting abandoned. No, wait! There was someone living there! Bayley's Creek flashed by, not as I remembered it, but now choked in willows and weeds, maybe the work of a beaver dam. Trees, larger than I recalled, seemed to crowd the highway. The hills looked more pedestrian, the dips and hollows less dramatic.

Settling in at the motel and then a casual stroll through my home village was something I hoped would prime me for a planned late breakfast, and then the evening ahead. It was still early, just past eight thirty, and few people were out, none of whom I recognized. The birds were pumping the air full of song; an occasional car left a wake of sound as it made its way along the main street; leaves fluttered in the morning sunshine.

But something was missing. Or different. Or not quite right.

Time soon went into high gear. Mid-morning, at nine thirty, we six friends from long ago gathered in the small restaurant by the bridge. There were smiles all round. Twinkles in the eye reflecting fond and wonderful memories. Recognition of faces and mannerisms. But recognition also of time's imprints on faces and bodies. There were handshakes, backslapping, and the usual rituals of news, catch-up, and kibitz ("You haven't changed at all! Hey! You old bastard! Where's your walker?"). There was laughing and reminiscing. Before I knew it, the day had already flown and we had reassembled for dinner: an outdoor barbecue, a large picnic table, beer, some wine, more laughter.

They all turned to greet me as I entered.

"Hey! Geoff!" Bobbie said. "Glad to see we didn't wear you out at breakfast", and he punched me playfully on the shoulder.

"Hi, Bobbie. It would take a lot more than you guys could muster to tire me out."

At this there was a general roar through beaming smiles. "The city slicker strikes back! Are you just going to stand there and take that Bobbie?"

I asked how the year had been.

"Fishermen!" Andy said. "The place was thick with them all year. Great custom but they ran us ragged!"

"And the cottage crowd!" Chuck drawled in his rich baritone voice. "Toilets. Broken pipes. Eaves. Leaky rooves. Put fifteen hundred miles on my truck. Never left the county."

There was a round of loud agreement, and beer glasses were raised in a common salute.

A few highlights from their year were tossed around. Eventually Bobbie turned to me, posed his question, to include me in the group when general politeness insisted that he wait no longer.

"And what about you? Still tinkering with equations, I bet." The others muttered varied repetitions on the same theme. I made evasive general responses on what I was up to, side-stepping any details. Any discussion of my working life would make me an intellectual intruder. It would be a turn-off, present to them a hill they wouldn't know how to climb. I learned that it had been a reasonable year for the fish bait and tackle business, that local plumbers had more jobs than they could manage, and that people doing odd jobs for the cottage crowd were worked off their feet.

It was just before sunset, I suppose, when the problem became evident to me. Not really the "problem", more the fact of competing image and reality.

As I looked around at my smiling and laughing boyhood friends, it was easy to see how time had sculpted new masks onto the adolescent features that I knew and still could recognize, how hairlines had been trimmed and modified, and how the shiny locks of youth had been dulled, thinned, and brushed in licks of white and silver. Their faces were leathery and roughened from years of sun and wind. There were lines and small nicks and scars where previously there had been none. Some eyes had gone slightly cloudy. The lithe and nimble forms of teenagers had been replaced by the solid and thickened bodies of middle-aged men. Their hands were hard and rough from physical labour. It was also easy to see how much my path had diverged from theirs.

But individual memories surfaced easily. Andy's vicious slapshot, and our many tired, languid, smiling highs in the dressing room after a hockey game won. Chuck's effortless and untiring paddle strokes during our canoe trips, and how each of us wanted him in our canoe. Wally's graceful dives off the bridge, and then his long-delayed resurfacing, causing panic among the adults who had stopped to watch. These were treasured things from the past. Events and scenes that had come and gone, leaving only traces of memory.

But somehow, for some reason, a single dominant recollection emerged, and I could see myself, once again, the guest invited to dinner at Bobbie's place after a day helping him cut his family's wood for the winter. It was an image different from the others, one that took a grip and remained. Their small kitchen and dining space always had that welcoming farmhouse warmth, chugged out over several hours by the large wood range squatting in the corner, where Bobbie's mom had cooked dinner. A kettle always sang atonally on the back of the wood stove, bringing to mind the aimless babble of chickens as they scratch in the dirt for seeds. Plates would be piled high in solid homely food, much of it pulled recently from the garden, and there would always be conversation around the table, about the Bakers' new extension, a house fire over at Kirkfield, or how George Henderson had split his trousers trying to heft too many bricks at once. The family's favourite dessert was blueberry pie, and it was served on the bottoms of the plates used for the main course. The catch here was that there would be no dessert unless the plate was wiped clean of main course and could be turned over without leaving blobs on the table cloth. Then there was a communal dishwashing chain gang. It was a family united against anything the world chose to throw at them.

All that was now faded, or at least far distant, reduced to sepia-tinged one-dimensional existence, but refusing to vanish entirely.

Or was I just remembering an elaborated pseudo-reality? Did my boyhood friends still enjoy timeless deep country rituals, things from a golden age that city dwellers would envy? Or were they themselves now just pale modern-day shadows, living the same diluted urban pipe dream of wannabe city types but transplanted uncomfortably, unsuitably, to the countryside — a pipe dream that, it seemed, so many people pretended to enjoy?

That was unfair. We had all traversed our timelines, courses marked by forks in the road, turning on decisions made by default or in the teeth of great uncertainty, often biased by poorly rooted preferences, sometimes influenced by fragments of ideology, always nudged along by family mythology, natural endowments, necessity, and just plain blind chance. It was my own life course through the austere lure of science and mathematics, that left me now feeling apart, somehow foreign, no longer belonging. But, most certainly, there had been a past: sunny, golden, and endless, even if it was not quite as I remembered it. And I suppose that's the main thing. Not to question some things too closely. Not to try to second guess, to corral, to mechanize, or to simplify our reality, which is far richer and more extensive than we humble beings can encompass.

At the end of the weekend, I would be going back to my world, to my engineering problems, my models, and to the fragments of interpretation handed to me from the past, from the Frenchman Clairaut, for example, who had ceased drawing breath more than two hundred and fifty years ago.

In the end, we really are such stuff as dreams are made of.

Another burst of hilarity erupted at the table. Looking around at the faces of my boyhood friends, I knew that our reality was here, not imagined, and we could choose to see past versions of it through a lens of kindly, uncritical recollection, and to create present versions using the hands we had been dealt. Or we could choose to discount the past and end up desperately unhappy, lost in space and time.

Bobbie looked across the table at me and flashed a blueberry-pie smile.

His Little Sweetheart

His grey suit had an elegant cut. About thirty-five, short dark brown hair, tall, and slim. The face was expressive but now somewhat clouded, his washed out blue eyes attractive, but just a bit bloodshot and displaying anxiety. The cream walls of the clinic, and the odour of disinfectant didn't help.

It was evident that he didn't want to be here.

He knew the feeling. He had lived long enough to be familiar with that dreadful coldness, the icy fingers of the adversary who would eventually defeat everyone.

He had known that something was badly wrong, had known for more than a week. He waited for the doctor to continue.

"It's in her liver. It's not a common tumour, but it's aggressive and fast-growing. Apart from palliative care, there's little we can do."

"But there must be something", he replied, almost in accusation.

"Yes, of course, and I didn't mean to say that we should do nothing. But of the several serious interventions we could undertake, all of them will be painful, will have unpleasant side effects, and, I have to say it, most probably will be unsuccessful. At best, we can hope for a few extra months of low-quality life."

He shook his head in a mixture of incomprehension, grief, and impotent pointless anger. "She's only eight years old!"

The doctor looked at him levelly. "Even one case like this is too many. And I see so many of them. If I could wish a cure into existence, believe me, I would drop everything today to do that."

He remained silent for a few moments. The doctor stood by, giving him time to absorb what she had told him, time to regain some mental balance, to begin taking some kind of measure of what he was about to lose. The doctor could read from his face what he was experiencing, having seen it so many times before. A hole was appearing — bottomless and permanent — where, just a few minutes, an hour ago, there had been none. Although he would find ways of living with it, it would remind him randomly, unexpectedly, over a long future, of the events of these few days, and inflict its pain all over again.

When she had been little, how playful she had been, mischievous, even devilishly so, and together they had invented dozens of games. She would eat with great concentration, and he had watched her for hours sometimes, as she slept.

It seemed that she was full of love, and she gave that love unconditionally. And he reflected, not for the first time, how astounding, how miraculous — yes, that's the word, *miraculous* — it was that such a small package could both attract and radiate so much love, could light so many bright candles in the world. And now her own candle, the source of all that joy and meaning, was being snuffed out.

"No", he said, with sudden and vehement decisiveness. "I want to make absolutely sure."

"I understand", the doctor said. "Please let me know."

He consulted at three other clinics. In just two days, he had the confirmation he had hoped against. Back at his home clinic, he and his doctor reviewed the situation again. After a long silence, the doctor spoke.

"You will probably want some time."

He nodded in pain and defeat.

Looking back at the doctor through his reverie, he said to himself that, yes, he really did want some time. He wanted lots of time. But it wasn't going to be given to him.

It was several minutes before he could speak again.

"I think heroic treatments are out of the question", he said. "Please tell me what we can do now."

The doctor nodded and began an explanation. But he really didn't hear all that much of it. He just continued looking at his little darling. She looked back, and he thought he could see understanding in her eyes. There was something else there as well, something that looked like ... what? That timeless wish à Dieu...

He stroked the top of her head, and the tears began running freely down his cheeks.

"Goodbye, my little sweetheart", he said and reverently touched her beautiful calico fur.

A story for Dusty.

On Foot Above the Clouds

At the start, there were fourteen of them. One wouldn't make it. Most of the other thirteen would have mixed experiences. Two would admit, if pressed, that they had been striving to expand a personal reality and they got much more out of it than they expected. Another two were searching futilely for escape, from just what he never learned, and he became convinced that they themselves didn't know. He was reminded of a distant cousin who, even in his final illness, continued hoping to "find himself".

The four women were all interesting, but they tended to stick together. With three of the men Benedict found that he had nothing in common. Two other men, Robert and Leslie, he warmed to right away.

The remaining one, although favoured in some ways, had still managed to become a piece of humanity's detritus. Having been moulded by the later decades of the twentieth century, this remaining fourteenth, who had the given name Wallace, somehow had lost access to that compartment labelled "Personal Meaning", probably during one of the irregular but frequent gyrations that it appeared his world had experienced. He had money, as he never tired of explaining to the others, but when that money was converted to the things he wanted, typically, BMWs, expensive watches, or the latest television or computer, novelty faded to dissatisfaction and disappointment within weeks, and soon the search was on for another diversion. He had seen the ad for this jaunt and had signed up right away, only later asking some basic questions.

Benedict himself undertook the trip with an open mind. He had always had a free-floating romantic attachment to the idea of the mountain, from pictures and stories. For him, it was an adventure, an intellectual and emotional trip. He had no intention to tick a box, or strike an item off what would now be called a "bucket list", a term that didn't exist back then.

From the moment their flight touched down in Arusha, Benedict found that the other-worldly presence of Africa began to take hold. The notions of time he had brought with him from the West grappled with the place he found himself in, and began to falter. In fewer than two days, a set of images had taken control of his view of the world: red soil that got into everything; disease — readily curable elsewhere but fatal here — burned indelible images; giant aloes; strange bugs that an entomophobe in the group referred to as a flying Cyclops; and curtains across Heaven's vault that were drawn or opened suddenly resulting in the almost instantaneous appearance of night and of day.

On the morning of the third day, the group had their first view of the objective: Kilimanjaro. Benedict recalled his map, but as he looked up at the mountain he could not distinguish Kibo, the peak they would be tackling, and also the highest of the three peaks that together are Kilimanjaro. From where they stood at that point, the three peaks all blended together, one great and graceful volcanic sweep up to the almost six-thousand-metre-high snowfields, from base to peak the tallest mountain in the world.

Benedict was sitting at a table on the patio behind the hotel, regarding the exotic trees waving in the light breeze and stark equatorial sunshine. But mostly, he was just feeling exhilarated at sitting in shade under the huge cascades of bougainvillea that tumbled over supports set around the patio. The mild disorientation of jetlag added to the tingle he felt at being, for the first time, in a part of the world where almost everything was new to him.

"Why are you doing this?" a voice asked.

Annoyed at least as much by the nature of the intrusion as by the intrusion itself, Benedict directed an expressionless stare at the interloper. He was about fifty and had attractive steel-grey hair and blue eyes that flitted about nervously, matching his fidgety body movements. Given what had brought them both to this place, Benedict was somewhat surprised at how heavy-set the man was — given the demands for exertion that lay ahead. Benedict recognized him immediately as Wallace. They had all become superficially acquainted before flying out to Africa, and having arrived, each of them soon determined which of his or her travelling companions would be worth the time and effort to get to know better. Benedict had quickly decided that Wallace was not worth the effort.

"Never been to this part of the world before", Benedict answered. "And it looked like an interesting challenge." Benedict didn't add that he had canvassed a couple of his friends to see what their reaction would be to the venture — had received a dismissive *Why the hell would anyone want to do that?* — and, somewhat perversely, that had clinched his own decision to sign up for the trip. A breeze caressed the bougainvillea overhead. Wallace fidgeted. His eyes flicked about, alighting on points of the panorama before him, but then jumping somewhere else before any appreciation of their previous point of focus could have formed.

"I have a list", Wallace said in sudden and unexplained emphasis. "Done well in business", he added, and nodded and smiled. "Lived all across the US and Canada. Decided I wanted something different." None of those statements seemed to invite a response, so Benedict took a long sip of the lemonade he had ordered from the bar inside. The richness of the vegetation laid out before him was highlighted by the tropical glare, and when combined with the still shimmering image of Kilimanjaro from that morning, it all confirmed for him that he was in the right place.

"Never been here before", Wallace bleated, sounding like someone pondering a major real estate purchase.

"You mean in Tanzania?"

"Where?"

"Tanzania. That's where we are now."

"Ah, right. Got it!"

Depends what "it" is, Benedict thought. There were a few moments of stilted silence, then Wallace brought his forearms down heavily onto the table.

"Got to go and wake up my broker", he barked. Then he rose and left.

Benedict relaxed, slid down slightly into his chair, and welcomed the return of companionable African solitude.

In front of him, two figures strolled into Benedict's field of vision, and he quickly recognized them as two of the climbing party —

Robert and Leslie, the two he had decided were the best candidates to become lasting companions by the end of the trip. They strolled over the grass and Benedict waved to them; there was a wave back, they picked up their pace, and soon were seated with Benedict at his table.

"Your time clocks getting readjusted?" Benedict asked.

"Pretty much", Leslie replied. "Just taking in the place."

Benedict looked at Robert, whose expression seemed a bit clouded.

"I have to admit to some discomfort", Robert said flatly.

Looks of inquiry from the other two invited him to elaborate.

"It's only, well, the amount I spent just to get here would be an unimaginable fortune to many of the local people I've seen."

Benedict and Leslie could only nod. They looked around at the richness and beauty of the landscape, a dramatic contrast to the human poverty they had all seen, and which Robert clearly found disturbing.

"I'm going to get a lemonade. You want one, Robert? Another, Benedict?"

Nods of acceptance sent Leslie off to the bar.

"What have you been up to?" Robert asked.

"Just having an orthogonal discussion with Gromit."

"What? Who?"

"Nothing. Just ignore me. I'm being gratuitously unkind."

Leslie returned with the three lemonades, they began talking about the approach to the climb, and it was clear they all shared the same excitement. The three of them then sat finishing their lemonades, waiting in interest to see the curtain of night descend once more with a sudden thud.

Breakfast was fresh papaya and a kind of bannock, at six thirty, then they brought their packs, containing only what was needed for the next six or seven days, to the hotel lobby. Bags and passengers piled into two aging VW vans for the short trip to the Kibo Hotel, a much more spartan accommodation that would be their starting and end point. Robert nudged Benedict and nodded toward one of the rear tires of their conveyance. Bald as an eagle was a serviceable description only if the eagle had cord showing on the top of its head. They got to the Kibo Hotel without either incident or tire failure, and everybody signed in to record the current date and the date of their expected return.

The guide, whose name was William Houghton was a Londoner and someone who Benedict judged to be about forty-five. William had done his homework, and knew the given names of everyone in the group. As he passed from one to another of them, checking water bottles, walking boots, walking sticks, and supplies of sunscreen, he moved with the grace and economy of one who is very fit. He wore gear that was as tough and veteran as he appeared to be himself, to which his trim figure, slight build, and sinewy forearms were testimony. His short black hair framed the edges of a surprisingly craggy face, something that seemed at odds with the warm and softly-spoken words of welcome and approval he directed at individuals.

When these preliminaries were complete, they all set off.

Within minutes, the path carried them into dense forest. Vines and mosses hung from massive trees. The calls of many different birds, all of them sounding large, filled the canopy above them. Monkeys hooted and cackled. There were frequent stops to take pictures, but then William urged them all to move on again. Presently the dense vegetation began to thin out, the trees became less massive, and within a few hours, they were in a sort of lush mixed forest. In due course, the soil cover became thinner, rocks began to show, and the trees became sparse and stunted. At mid-afternoon, they reached Mandara Hut, where they would spend the first night in sturdy pine A-frame cabins, each set on a concrete slab and having space for eight people. They all slipped off their backpacks, looked around the open stony area, and began the unconscious self-selection as to who would be in which huts. The guide pointed off to his right, indicating the direction to the mountain. "But at this time of day", he explained, "it's always obscured by cloud".

Around seven thirty, it would suddenly become dark. There would be nothing to do then but go to bed. But that was still a few hours away. They had their evening meal, then sat on the steps of two adjacent huts. There was some talk of the day just passed, some talk of the next day, but most of the climbers were silent, reviewing the mental images they had amassed thus far. Wallace announced suddenly that his left foot hurt, at which William had Wallace remove his boot and sock, and told him to bathe the foot in water and to leave it bare during the night.

It took barely fifteen minutes for the late afternoon sky to empty completely of light. A full spread of stars appeared, and Benedict and Leslie sat up for a further half hour talking about everything and nothing. The next morning they agreed that even that had been a mistake. Because there had been no moon, and because it was pitch black inside the huts, the cost of finding their bunks had been a stubbed toe, two barked shins, and a cracked noggin.

The somewhat bleary-eyed group gathered for breakfast as a loose huddle in decidedly chilly air. There was morning mist, but somewhere behind it the sun was working hard. The guide clapped his hands several times.

"You all slept well, I see." A brief ironic smile.

"We have a few minutes more for breakfast, so take your time." He then primed them for the day's hike. "We'll be taxed a little more today than yesterday. The distance we have to cover is about fifty percent greater and we'll be climbing to about 3,700 metres. There might seem to be no need for it now, but please smear on your sunscreen. And check that your water bottles are full.

"One final but important item. Make sure you use the facilities before we leave", and he pointed to one forlorn and uninviting outhouse. "There will be few if any shrubs along the way today, so if Nature calls you'll need to answer in plain view. We need to stick together, so no wandering off to take a leak in private."

He looked around, expecting and seeing the reality of their situation register on the group's faces. "Any questions?" Another look around and a smile of encouragement. "Okay. We'll strike out in ten minutes."

At a sign from William they shouldered their packs and headed off along the path, which began ascending almost immediately.

Within an hour, Benedict noticed that two of the group had slightly laboured breathing, and he recalled the advice he had received back home from seasoned hikers and from his doctor. The hikers had all said that preparation would be essential: lots of long-distance walking to become accustomed to daylong exertion, a good deal of distance running to build up leg muscles, oxygen-carrying capacity, and gamma globulin. His doctor was taken aback when Benedict asked whether he should have a preventive appendectomy; he gave Benedict's abdomen a thorough examination and expressed the judgment that there was nothing wrong with him and that the risk of an appendectomy now was probably greater than the risk of appendicitis over the eight days on the mountain. However, one of the hikers he had consulted told Benedict that he should be very careful while he was up there. There would be no air evacuation possible, the consequence of a serious leg fracture while he was on the mountain most likely would be an unpleasant and gangrenous end to his life, and that in any case, Benedict did not want to find himself in an African hospital, no matter what the reason.

The second night's camp was located at Horombo Hut. By then Wallace's breathing was ragged, and two others were struggling. It was also the first point at which Benedict noticed that even modest effort raised his own breathing rate, although once the effort ceased, his breathing tailed off to normal in about twenty seconds. It was the first time he had felt these effects of altitude.

The ground at Horombo was rougher and rockier than at the previous camp. The guide placed his backpack on one of the centrally placed picnic tables, and encouraged everyone to gather round.

"Good job today everyone. We're now more than halfway up the mountain. This camp", and he waved at the huts, "is similar to the one yesterday. Over there", and he pointed to a distant and lonely outhouse, "is the usual lack of running water, hot or cold." There were a few light chuckles.

"We'll eat soon. You have all noticed that the sun sets early here, and night comes on quickly. That's good because we need a good sleep tonight. Tomorrow will be a taxing day as well."

He looked around at the group.

"I'm sure that you've also noticed that breathing became more difficult during the day. The air's getting thinner. It's nothing to worry about. It just means that as we go higher we need to take things more slowly."

William looked around again.

"One more important thing. Horombo is in rugged terrain. I don't want to alarm anyone, but there are some cliffs and steep drops around us. So please don't go wandering off. Especially when it's dark. Okay?"

Once more, William looked around.

"Well", he began and a hint of a smile appeared, "I'd love to invite you to join me for a drink, but… we'll get together for dinner instead." Then he smiled, picked up his backpack and walked to one of the huts.

Benedict, Leslie, and Robert gathered again for a chat before the evening meal. They agreed that tonight there would be no staying up after sundown. A taxing day tomorrow, William had warned. After their experience of the day just passed, they took that warning seriously. Robert was quiet, but Benedict sensed that he wanted company, discussion.

"So far so good?" Benedict asked.

"Yes…", Robert replied. "Although I'm finding it an eye-opener."

"How so?"

"Well, in many senses. I hadn't counted on the area being so dramatic. The mountain. The trees. The grasses. And the flowers in Arusha!"

"Yes. Impressive." But Benedict felt that something more pithy was coming.

"I took a tour around Arusha, and a couple of nearby villages", Robert said.

Benedict nodded but didn't comment.

"The people are very attractive, handsome. And cheerful. Colourful clothes." A pause. "I saw them haggling and bartering in the markets."

Another longer pause.

"But it was the disease. Leprosy. Other things", and Benedict got the strong sense that Robert was seeing all this again in his mind.

They talked some more. Robert was obviously disturbed at what he had seen.

"I know that it's silly to judge what's here by what we have", Robert continued. "But their dwellings… very basic. It seems that the use of night soil is common. I guess that life in general is… well, basic."

Their discussion continued for another ten minutes. Benedict drew out Robert on his own past. It soon became evident that this was Robert's first look at a poor society. A humanist, Benedict thought, someone who feels the deprivation of others personally and strongly.

When dinner was ready, they all found places to sit and eat. There was little conversation. Everyone was tired and strained by the day. William came over and sat next to Benedict. He had come here to

Tanzania, he told Benedict, after stumbling upon a short article entitled "An African Arcadia" in the August 1886 issue of *The Eclectic Magazine of Foreign Literature, Science and Art*. The article recounted a history of the first encounters of Europeans with the mountain.

"How long have you been here?" Benedict asked.

"Oh, it's, let's see, almost twenty-five years."

"So you came out as a young man."

Nod.

"What prompted you to stay?"

After a long pause, William said "I'd been here not quite a year when I realized how little I missed London. In fact, I didn't miss it at all."

Benedict waited to see whether William would say anything further, and after a moment he did continue.

"Maybe it's because of my own background as part of a colonizing country, but… I became interested in the history of the place right away. And the place itself. I came to love it. It really is Arcadia."

William had another mouthful of food and took a sip from his drinking cup. He turned to look at Benedict.

"I became an ecologist. Not just an activist. I studied the place. There are dozens of ecosystems. All in this small space. Great diversity. Rivals anything anywhere else on the planet."

Another drink of water.

"What about the people?" Benedict asked.

"Got to know them too, of course. Had to. The language and the customs. You might find it hard to believe, but the people here are sophisticated. I like them."

They talked some more about William's work as a park guide. He spoke about how many climbers came here, how he had set up an arrangement with about forty other guides to try to make sure that the income from those visitors is spread around, not siphoned off.

"So you plan to stay here?" Benedict asked.

"Yes. I don't see myself leaving anytime soon. But, who knows…"

Benedict and William lapsed into silence for a moment, each of them looking at some feature of Africa, but also at inner visions.

"I think Wallace won't be able to go beyond Horombo", William said without any lead-in. "He's probably twenty pounds overweight for this kind of venture. He's going to have a lot more trouble as the air gets thinner, and I'm afraid that if he hikes another ten miles, the blisters on his right foot could become infected. I have some cream I've put on them, but…"

"What will he do?" Benedict asked. "Surely he can't just start back down on his own!"

"Oh, good God no! There's a group coming down who will be overnighting here tomorrow. He can wait here during the day, spend tomorrow night and go back down with them."

"Have you spoken to him about this?"

"Not yet."

"Do you mind if I speak to him?"

"No, not at all. But why would you? I sense that you don't like him."

"I don't. None of our group does. But he shouldn't think we don't care."

William nodded.

There was about forty-five minutes of daylight left, and Benedict walked over and sat down next to Wallace.

"How's it going?" he began.

"Fine, fine. Looking forward to tomorrow's hike."

"Not having too much trouble breathing?"

"Breathing? No! Why should I? It's just the altitude. No big deal."

"Foot doing all right?"

"Sore, but okay."

Wallace turned to look more closely at Benedict. A flicker of suspicion appeared on his face.

"I'm not really sure why you're asking all these questions."

"Well, we're all in this together, Wa—"

"We're not all in it together. That's just a bunch of bleeding-heart liberal twaddle. Each of us is here because we've accepted our own personal challenges."

"You're probably partly right in that. I know that I have my own objectives for this trip. What are you looking forward to tomorrow?"

"Oh, just more of the same. Comparing myself to others. Maybe seeing the body of a tiger."

Benedict smiled in some surprise at what he took to be a capricious literary allusion coming from Wallace.

"You're a fan of Hemingway?"

"Damn right I am. There was a real man's man."

Benedict was taken aback, but managed not to show it, although he looked sharply at Wallace. "But he blew his head off with a shotgun."

Wallace shook his own head vigorously. "It was an accident. That whole story was just more bleeding-heart liberal defamation of a great individual."

Benedict wasn't going to argue the point, but he knew otherwise. Having been an admirer of Hemingway after studying *The Old Man And The Sea* as a teenager, his outlook became much more ambivalent the more he had learned about the man.

Benedict put his hands on his knees, preparing to lever himself to his feet, and he turned and smiled at Wallace. "Okay. See you in the morning." But Wallace said nothing in return, scowled, and shifted so that he was facing away from Benedict.

There was nothing more to say. Benedict shrugged, rose, and walked away. People had collected in small groups. Benedict went to join Leslie, who was cleaning some caked mud from his hiking boots. They chatted about nothing in particular.

From the corner of his eye, Benedict noticed William rise and begin walking toward Wallace. He sat next to Wallace and they began talking. Without any warning, there were raised voices.

"There's no way I'm staying here! I paid to get to the top of this mountain and I'm damn well gonna do just that!"

"You are staying here, Mr. Davis. You're my responsibility while we're up here, and I remind you that you signed papers agreeing to accept my authority. You'll wait here tomorrow and go back down the following day with the group that's descending. I'm not going to argue about it. That's what will happen."

"It's that bastard Howells, isn't it? He put you up to this!"

"Sir, nobody has put me up to anything, and Mr. Howells has not influenced my decision in any way. Your foot is blistered and inflamed. You won't make it tomorrow. It'll be difficult enough for you to make it back down. You're staying here tomorrow. And that's the end of the matter."

"And if I refuse to do that? If I come along anyway?"

"In that case, Mr. Davis, I will take the entire group back down the mountain, you will be reported to the park authorities, and I would fully expect that you will be fined."

All other conversation had ceased abruptly. Heads had turned. There were expressions of surprise and disapproval. Whatever sympathy there might have been for Wallace evaporated quickly enough. In the end, he backed down with very ill grace.

Showing what Benedict thought to be considerable understanding and humanity, William convinced Wallace to let him take another look at Wallace's foot, he applied more cream, and placed another dressing on the blistered area. It was a sombre and silent group that drifted off to their huts for the night.

The next morning, William roused Wallace and showed him a set of instructions he had written out to cover the time between our group's heading off on the next stage and the descending group reaching Horombo. William and Wallace both signed the instructions and William took the duplicate set with him. There was food and water left for Wallace, who sat at his table, his body language aggressive. Leslie and Benedict had shouldered their backpacks and stopped next to Wallace on the way past. Benedict began to speak.

"I'm sorry things worked out this way for you—"

Wallace turned on them.

"Just fuck off up your mountain!" he shouted.

Leslie and Benedict hesitated briefly, then joined the others, and the group of thirteen set off from Horombo without looking back.

The sun was hot by nine thirty, beating down from a cloudless sky. The air was dry, the ground was dusty, and from it protruded clumps of dead brown grass. During the day, William moved regularly from the front to the rear of the column of hikers, making sure they were okay, offering encouragement when it seemed to be needed. He turned now to face them at the head of the group.

"Everyone okay?"

Affirmative murmurs.

"Please make sure you take some water regularly. I suggest a large mouthful about every hour. But you can see that everything here is dry. We have some distance to go before we can refill our canteens. So don't empty them too quickly. If you find that you're thirsty and out of water, please let me know."

The surroundings soon became dominated by huge, impressive, and beautiful xerophytic plants and expanses of dry grass. It seemed that their progress was non-existent. The Saddle, that flattish area between the towering heights of Kibo and Mawenzi peaks, gave the impression of having an almost infinite expanse. But at the same time, it was exhilarating. To the right, the jagged features of Mawenzi soared above them. To the left, the higher and more substantial mass of Kibo offered its silent challenge. Because that was where they were going.

There were several rest stops, William not allowing them more than about ten minutes at each, and it was here that they all first noticed an effect that would become much more pronounced higher up. It surprised Benedict, the difficulty of hauling himself up from a relaxed sitting position to his feet at the end of the rest stop. Bits of exposed skin were sticky from generous latherings of sunscreen, but although the sun felt fiercely hot, the air was cold. Slowly, Mawenzi slid past on their right, the trail moved off in a long slow bend to the left and followed an increasing gradient that rose before them. Everyone was breathing fairly heavily now, including the two who barely would manage ultimately to make it to the top, both of them now sucking air in great gasps. Benedict checked his pulse. What would normally have been in the low sixties for this stately pace back home was now in the high eighties.

Gradually, the xerophytic plants disappeared. Then the grass thinned out and vanished as well. Conversation had tailed off, then ceased. It was extra effort that everybody was more than willing to avoid. At about four o'clock in the afternoon, they could see a small structure ahead and above them.

"Kibo Hut", William said.

"We all sleep in one hut tonight?" someone asked.

"Yes", William replied. "Sort of."

Their approach to the hut seemed impossibly slow, but its features began to resolve, and then the stone construction of the hut became evident. Most people dropped their packs in relief, sat down heavily leaning against the hut wall, and looked back the way they had come. They were surrounded now by rocks and scree fields. No plants or grasses were anywhere in sight. Within a few minutes, William had passed around metal mugs of warm, weak, very sweet tea. The day's final meal was packed rations that everyone chewed on mechanically.

William laid out the plan for the next and final stage of the ascent. At some level, everyone was aware already of how this final stage would unfold, having been briefed both at home and in the hotel before they had started the first day of walking. They would awaken at midnight and begin their final climb then. Despite the fact that they were now where they were and not in some plush hotel, and that they could now see the reality confronting them, this statement about striking out again at midnight brought barely a flicker of response. Looking around, Benedict recognized exhaustion, the effect of chronic oxygen debt, on otherwise alert faces. People began drifting off into the hut to find a place to sleep even before the sun had set. Fastidiousness over sleeping arrangements was swept aside, and women and men bunked down wherever they found space.

Benedict awoke with a very sudden start, almost a feeling of panic. Looking at his watch, he was astonished to realize that although it was barely eight thirty, everything was pitch black. Less than half an hour later, he jolted awake again, and this pattern repeated throughout their half night. After the third such panicked awakening, he began seeking the cause. There was no noise. Outside, no wind blew. There were no animals about. Utter silence, that disturbing silence of an anechoic room, prevailed. He checked his pulse and found to his astonishment and alarm, that it was over ninety. He checked again. Same result.

Thin air.

Kibo Hut is at fifteen thousand feet. Benedict realized that most of the atmosphere was now below him. His lungs, heart, and vascular system were working overtime to scavenge the little oxygen available and deliver it to meet the clamouring demands of his body. As he drifted off to sleep, his breathing slowed, an oxygen debt built up, and he was jolted awake to take deep breaths and pay down the debt. It was one of the most uncomfortable, but in an odd way intriguing, nights he had ever spent.

His disorientation was virtually complete when he was shaken awake in total darkness. He heard William's voice. And although he knew it was William, for some odd reason he wondered where he was. Other people were moving about. There were murmurs and groans. They had slept in their boots because it might well have been impossible to find boots, put them on the correct feet, and tie them up in complete darkness. Benedict had used his pack as a pillow, worn his coat as a blanket, as had the others. Soon enough, they were outside, shivering in that distinctive way that follows a partial night of chilled and inadequate sleep. In what seemed an absurd contradiction to the way they all felt, a sky full of stars smiled down upon them, and under that faint glow, they began their march up the path that followed a switchback route across the scree. William carried the only flashlight, and he used it occasionally to check that the group was staying together.

Their marching orders for the next six hours were clear: Stay as close to the person in front of you as you can. Walking will be difficult. Don't leave the path. Keep your eyes on your feet. Take short steps. Don't try to take more than one step per second. Don't try looking up to see how far there is to go.

At half past midnight, they struck out. Benedict was a mass of mixed emotions — he felt the thrill of beginning the final phase of the ascent and, each time he heard someone retch, the fear that he wouldn't make it; he was exhausted from lack of sleep and weak from lack of oxygen, and a slight disorientation and dizziness came over him occasionally. He had images of the peak, of being back down and in a shower, the periodic jag of mild panic when his footing slipped on the scree. He was in another world. Things were different. And he felt a bit like an infant, not able to respond quickly enough or in the right way when something changed. The chill they all felt as they set off vanished quickly. Heavy breathing was heard. Benedict checked his pulse a few minutes after they had set out. It was well over one hundred. He began feeling warm and unzipped his jacket. Every five minutes or so, the path went through a sharp hairpin.

Occasionally a piece of scree slid off and rattled down the slope, reminding everyone that they were on the edge of a fairly steep and quite unstable gradient. The mild throbbing in Benedict's head, which had been there since he had been shaken awake, grew more intense, and within an hour had turned into an irritating headache. The only sounds were the crunch of feet on stone and the clank of walking sticks. The faint starlight was just enough, Benedict thought, to allow him to get a shadowy glimpse of his own feet.

Left foot down. Push. Right foot down. Push. Repeat. Repeat. Repeat.

He could sense rather than see the person in front of him, had no idea who it was, whether male or female. Right foot down…

More than once the thought broke through to his consciousness — *I wonder how far we have left to go* — but he resisted the urge to look up, knowing that most likely, the faint starlight would reveal, cruelly, a steep, indefinitely long, depressing sweep of slope, the upper end of it not discernable, leading to…

Left foot down. Right foot down. Repeat. Repeat. Repeat.

Benedict dragged out into consciousness the words of a song entitled "Morgen". Being in German, this took some effort. He began hearing the music alongside, and then he went back to the beginning of the song and played it through at the tempo he remembered.

Ivo Robić. That was who had sung it.

Benedict let the song sing itself in his head. Stumbled a little over some of the words. The song unfolded again in his mind, two or three times more.

Then suddenly another song burst in — "Ce Que Je Crains" — and he could hear the voice of Alain Barrière and the sweet piano background. The words of that song unwound in his head as well. And again. And again.

Another fist-sized piece of rock tumbled off to his left, and then began its long and alarming descent, reminding him once more that he had to keep his mind at least half on what he was doing.

Left foot down. Right foot down.

"I can't … I can't…" And then some sobbing.

"It's not far now", William said softly.

"I can't…"

Benedict recognized that it was Kathy, one of the four women on the trip. He thought briefly about stopping, helping Kathy up, but then realized in frustration and impatience, that he was barely strong enough to push himself forward. Besides, that was why there was a guide, and he knew far more about what to do, when, and why, than any of them.

"Everyone stop please", William said. "Just hold your positions."

Benedict could hear William speaking softly to Kathy. In a few moments she stopped sobbing. In a few moments more, she rose to her feet with William's help, Benedict could hear her say 'Okay' a couple of times, then William asked everyone to resume the ascent.

Four more hairpins came and went. The effort to keep moving was becoming ... but he clamped down on that thought.

For a time, Benedict counted. He tried to count what he thought were seconds. Got to one thousand. Lost track. Started over again, got to two thousand four hundred that time. The sounds of the others ahead of him and behind him filled his world. Heavy breathing. The occasional cough. Multiple retches at one point. Murmurs. Gradually, all this became filtered out. Benedict retreated within himself. His thought, his rapid pulse, his regular steps, the clank of his walking stick on the scree — these became his world.

His legs needed reminding.

Left foot down. Right foot down. Left foot down.

"Boots, boots, boots, boots marching over Africa..."

Left foot down. Keep your balance, he reminded himself for perhaps the fortieth time. For God's sake, don't drop the walking stick. Keep close to the person in front, the red jacket, the white socks, the tan boots, the...

The red jacket!

Benedict checked his watch.

Twenty past five.

That's why he could tell the jacket was red. It was early morning. They had been struggling up this slope for five hours.

Benedict raised his head, looked up, in the direction they were heading.

There it was. About two hundred metres ahead. A line where the slope met a grey sky that had already begun to wash out the stars.

Twenty minutes later, he reached the top of Kilimanjaro. Well, reached Gilman's Point. The top of Kibo is Uhuru, slightly higher and a few hundred metres away, and in another half hour he was there.

Benedict returned to Gilman's Point, where the majority of the group had stopped, found a spot and sat heavily. His head thudded dully. He felt slightly nauseous, but knew that he wouldn't be sick. Just then he heard the sound of retching somewhere to his right. His breathing was deep and rapid, and slowed only slightly, even after a few minutes of resting. He checked his heart rate: just over a hundred and holding.

Leslie and Robert joined him. They all exchanged crooked smiles and shook hands in silent but eloquent mutual congratulation.

The sky was now full of light, and they looked out from their perch, a little more than 19,000 feet up. Below them, several thousand feet below, lay a thin blanket of cloud, broken in enough spots to see images of land far beneath.

There was a flash as the sun peeked over the horizon. The undersides of the clouds below them were suddenly washed in pink. There was nothing to say, and the three of them sat and watched for almost half an hour. When the sun rose above the cloud blanket, William announced that they had to start making their way back down, even though it was not yet eight o'clock.

"Ninety percent of the atmosphere is below us, and when the sun gets a bit higher in the sky, the UV will come straight in. We need to get some air above us in the next few hours. And the sun soon warms the sides of the mountain. Moist air is heated and drawn upwards. At this altitude, the moisture condenses."

The significance of William's explanation was clear. Fog. They didn't want to be peering through fog as they made their way back down. Benedict remembered at Mandara Hut, William pointing toward the mountain, and nobody being able to see it because it was shrouded in cloud.

Two surprises awaited Benedict.

He had been seated there at Gilman's for more than half an hour. It took an astonishing effort, a supreme and unimaginable effort of will just to stand up. *This isn't good. I've used my last resources to get up here. I'm screwed now.*

But they all started back down. In just a couple of hours, they passed Kibo Hut and moved out onto the long stretch of The Saddle. But now, on the way back down, things were different. And this was the second surprise.

They gambolled like calves.

Armies of red-blood-cell reservists had been called to duty from their barracks in the spleen. These sucked up oxygen. For many weeks afterwards, Benedict could remember the precise feeling, the sense of elation, as strength and life flowed generously back into his body. Arms and legs moved in increasing strength and co-ordination. There was a real urge to skip and dance along the path. Benedict found that powerful sense of exhilaration overwhelming and difficult to describe, then, and even today.

They spent nights at Horombo and Mandara, then made the final leg of descent to the Kibo Hotel the next morning. Their first shower in six days was luxury. In what they all learned had become something of a tradition, a group of about twenty locals, all young men, gathered in the common area of the hotel, welcomed them back, sang a song about Kilimanjaro, and then were rewarded by the climbers in the form of free beer. I noticed Robert going around to the locals with our guide and getting into quite long discussions. Leslie and I sat in a corner and talked about the climb.

"It wasn't just the climb", Leslie said, "at least not for me. I think I can see what attracts our guide to this place. It's a brilliant example of what our world is all about." A little more than three years later, Leslie self-published a book entitled *On Foot Above the Clouds*.

"What about you?" Leslie asked.

Benedict took his time replying.

"It's been a life experience, but I need to think about it more."

Leslie nodded.

"I can tell you what it wasn't, though", Leslie said. "Not for me. It wasn't a hook for hanging bullshit statements like 'learning what I'm made of', 'going through the pain of hell', 'finding and exceeding human limits', and God knows how much other crap I've read from people who've made this trip."

To Benedict, this statement was a surprise, coming from Leslie, a man he had learned to regard as mild-mannered.

"It's been humbling, I would say", Benedict added at length.

They both sat in reverie.

Then Benedict roused himself. "I wonder where Wallace is."

"Ah, yes", Leslie said in some interest, and looking around quickly, he waved to their guide in a gesture that invited William to join them.

The three of them sat and clinked their beer glasses.

"How many times have you taken groups up Kilimanjaro?" Benedict asked.

"This was my fifty-fourth trip."

"Must be boring by now, or at least routine."

"Far from it", William replied. "Each time I go up I realize how little I really know about the place."

They chatted a bit more, then Leslie asked about Wallace.

William's expression collapsed, then his eyes squinted and his features hardened.

"Has something happened?" Leslie asked.

"He's dead", William said expressionlessly.

Shocked silence.

"How?"

"Nobody saw. I warned him at least four times to be careful at Horombo. He was waiting when the descending group reached the camp. The guide for that group confirmed that he had spoken to Wallace, told him how and when they would start making the descent to Mandara and then to the Kibo Hotel."

William looked off into the distance for a long while, fiddling with a button on his shirt sleeve.

"When it came time for the evening meal, they couldn't find him. The guide and two others went off to search. Just before the light failed, they spotted his body on a ledge about fifty metres down. He was dead, had been for some time."

William looked into the distance and his expression hardened once more. "Shit", he said under his breath.

"Will there be some sort of investigation?" Benedict asked.

"Already done", William said, still in the same monotone. "A senior park official came up first thing next morning, took photos, interviewed everyone, and then they recovered the body and carried it back down to park headquarters. It's in the morgue in Arusha."

"What do they think happened?" Leslie asked.

William shrugged. "An accident. Wallace probably went too close to the edge, lost his balance…

"But", William continued, "after the descending group had arrived at Horombo, two of them said Wallace was behaving oddly".

Leslie and Benedict glanced at each other. William caught the unspoken message.

"I know, I know", he said. "Yes, Wallace was something of an odd guy. So behaving oddly…"

"What was it specifically that they considered odd?" Benedict asked.

"Wallace kept mumbling something about stock quotes. And he said something about seeing a light airplane circling."

"A light airplane?" Leslie said in surprise. "Is that common out here?"

"No. Not at all. In fact it almost never happens. The mountain can generate sudden air currents that are dangerous for a light plane if it flies too close to the sides of the mountain."

They gazed at empty beer glasses, and Benedict quietly signalled for three more. The beers arrived in less than a minute. William sat looking disconsolately at his glass. But suddenly he raised his head and looked at the other two.

"Do either of you have any idea what he might have been talking about, this airplane business?"

"No. None at all", Leslie said and took a small sip of beer.

"Yes", Benedict said quietly after a few moments of silence.

They both turned to focus intently on Benedict.

"Well, I can't be sure", Benedict said. "Before we began the ascent, I took some time to speak to Wallace. He had made no friends among the rest of the group, and I thought I might ... I don't know ... Anyway, Wallace mentioned to me that he thought we might find a dead tiger on the way up the mountain, and—"

"A dead tiger?" William exclaimed in puzzlement, looking back and forth between Benedict and Leslie. "What would — oh, shit! Surely not Hemingway?"

"Yes", Benedict said. "Wallace considered him a great man, a real man's man, he called him. In that context, the light plane makes some kind of twisted sense. You know, the last pages of Hemingway's short story, 'The Snows of Kilimanjaro'. I read it just before I came out here."

They talked about Wallace a bit more. William asked for details, questioned Benedict closely, took several pages of notes, then went off to find a park official.

Dinner was a quiet affair. Leslie and Benedict sat together, apart from the rest of the group. Robert had been expansive all afternoon about something, and now was off somewhere talking to someone.

"A penny?" Leslie said, after more than five minutes of silence had settled between them.

"Oh, just wondering idly about Wallace."

"Hmmm."

Benedict sat thinking. About the basic sadness that seemed to surround Wallace. About parallels to the contradiction that was Hemingway. About how people become trapped in ideologies.

"He was a strange one", Leslie added at length. "But nobody deserves that sort of end."

"No", Benedict replied. "But he was more than just strange. I think he was a tortured soul. Very successful financially. Right-wing attitudes to match. But there seemed to be very little in his life that had true meaning. I think he was just an unhappy man."

"Do you think he…?" Leslie began.

Benedict just looked ahead into space.

"On Foot Above the Clouds" draws on the author's own experience of his ascent of Kilimanjaro in 1983, and on elements in Ernest Hemingway's short story "The Snows of Kilimanjaro".

Elevator Etiquette

On Fridays, I muse. Last Friday, while musing on aeroplanes, and railway carriages, among other things, a man interrupted my thoughts.

"Excuse me", he began nervously. "I think there's something wrong with this elevator."

He was short, fiftyish, and gave rapid sideways glances at whatever drew his attention. I had seen him before in the building but knew nothing about him. He was eminently forgettable, and right now he was badly frightened. Sweat glistened on his brow and upper lip; in one hand he had twisted a glove into a grotesque half nelson; his other hand clutched the small rail on the elevator wall in a white-knuckled death grip.

"Oh? In what way?" I asked.

This was, to be honest, a naive question, because the lights on the indicator panel above the doors had gone out, we didn't know what floor we were passing, and the elevator was moving slowly with sudden downward jerks.

After flicking several more nervous glances at me, he cleared a dry throat and said a bit too loudly, "Do you think we should call for help?"

My first thought was that he could easily reach for the telephone in its little brass box next to the emergency button and call for help himself. Then I realized that he didn't dare let go of the railing. His type was familiar to me. One finds people like him in aeroplanes, but not in railway carriages. What I mean is that they are quite evident in aeroplanes. Their fear pervades the cabin for several seats in each direction. Sweat stands out in beads on their faces at take-off and landing, during periods of turbulence, at the sight of thunder cells (no matter how distant), and even on overhearing frivolous remarks — for instance, "Why do you suppose there's a hole out there in the wing?" In railway carriages, these people blend with the upholstery, say nothing, and become invisible for all social purposes.

They are to be pitied, because railway carriages are perhaps the best places to meet people. This is particularly so in the European carriages, which are divided into compartments. There isn't the problem of crowds, one can exchange sections of newspaper, and there is usually relaxing and interesting scenery to remark upon: hares starting from the trackside, cattle watching uncertainly as the train passes, donkeys munching thistle in bliss and ignorance.

My companion cleared his throat again, bringing me back to a late Friday afternoon in an elevator. But I had found a point worth pursuing.

Ignoring his outstanding query, I countered with a question of my own. "Why do you think that elevators are unlikely places to meet people?" I turned to look at him. "Of course, one doesn't expect to spend hours in them, but even so, nobody says a thing when they enter an elevator. Don't you find that odd?"

He took my conversational gambit in the wrong sense altogether, casting me a glance such as a beleaguered brigadier might on being told that the enemy has opened a second front. He did not reply, because at that moment the elevator began to pick up speed, and soon we were descending normally. My companion's moray-like grip on the railing relaxed, and he smiled wanly, at the same time rolling his eyes indulgently at the imperfections of our technological society and the dullard engineers who fashion it.

This was a mistake. The kindly spirit that guided Thomas Telford and I. K. Brunel may well have taken umbrage. The elevator decelerated suddenly and stopped. The light on the indicator panel came on briefly, showing that we were at the thirty-sixth floor. A buzzer sounded somewhere distantly in the building. The elevator began to rise, slowly.

At this, my companion was transformed into a virtual factory of adrenaline. He clutched the railing ferociously, raising the stress in it almost to the plastic flow region.

"Oh, bother", I sighed.

He responded immediately this time, with alarm and outrage. "Bother? We might be killed!"

"Surely that's a bit melodramatic", I observed sceptically. "You realize, don't you, that elevators are perfectly safe. Nothing can happen to us besides some slight inconvenience."

He did not look convinced. His glove was dead. A seam had opened on the index finger. It was time to do the humane thing. Although not a Marxist, I reasoned that the truth might help to free him from the thrall of his anxieties.

"The trouble today", I began, "is that people take things too much for granted. They never stop to think about things, like elevators. And I would wager that if asked what made the greatest impression on their lives, most people would list entirely trivial items: cake mixes, fibre-reinforced golf clubs, early ripening tomatoes. What about elevators? Without elevators there would be no tall buildings. Our cities would be transformed; buildings would only be tall enough to allow the average worker to carry a photocopy machine to the top floor. Traffic patterns would be radically different; our lives would be utterly changed. Without tall buildings there would be no mid-town canyons, no gale force winds, no huddle of banks and their executive eyries. The pressure on land values would be much reduced. Elevators are one of the main reasons for the high price of houses today."

He was transfixed, but I couldn't tell whether he was genuinely interested in the subject or immobilized by fear. *May as well take the hopeful view…*

"There's another side to them though, enrapturing for the mechanically minded. They are exceptionally interesting machines with long pedigrees. Vitruvius wrote about elevating devices. Did you know that at one time, elevators were driven by steam? Dates back to the late eighteenth century, that one, but it is true that the first steam passenger elevator didn't appear until 1857 — Haughwout Department Store, New York City. There were a couple here in Toronto, as well. One in a building up near Yorkville Avenue, I think. Hardly Flash Gordon stuff, though. Four or five storeys a minute, and a lot of hissing and clanking. And you probably didn't know that the early elevator cages were suspended on hempen ropes? Not very reliable."

True, I was being a shade unreasonable. My companion had probably had a hard week. I could scarcely expect him to take in so much information at once. Little wonder that his expression was blank. Regardless, I decided to continue.

"It's just because they're so ordinary, so uninspiring, that people don't think twice about elevators. If they did, if they took the time to inform themselves, they would be amazed at how far we've come. Take the cables that are holding us up right now: high-quality steel, regularly maintained and inspected, a healthy safety factor."

I paused here to consider where my thoughts were leading: the impromptu philosopher adjusting his loincloth.

To this moment, the elevator had been rising slowly, but now it stopped and waited, almost as if listening to my address, waiting for the next gyration in logic.

I came, at last, to the most comforting part of my topic. "Elevators also have fail-safe systems, powerful jaws that are held open by the weight of the elevator itself. If anything should happen, like a broken cable, those jaws would snap shut on the guide rails and hold the elevator where it was. In fact, it was just this kind of demonstrated safety that made elevators thinkable on the large scale. Without mechanisms of that sort, people would be plunging to their deaths every day."

As if to give the lie to my discourse, the elevator suddenly lurched earthwards, and my companion's expressionless face collapsed into a pit of dread. His mouth opened slowly into a round black hole, releasing a small squeak. The work of Edvard Munch came to mind. Our speed increased. The buzzer was sounding again, and it gave a sad Doppler farewell as we passed it. There was an audible hiss outside the carriage. With great effort, my companion swivelled his head on an almost petrified neck, to direct at me his full panic.

"Counterweights", I reassured him. "Possibly something to do with the compensating cable. You need one of those in some types of elevator to keep a constant torque on the motor." My strategy was to keep a steady flow of reassuring factual information moving in his direction; but we just weren't communicating effectively.

"If you're uncomfortable, try swallowing. By the way, that's really the only limitation on the speed of elevators. Descending faster than about thirty-five feet per second puts too much strain on the human ear. Can't adjust that fast with comfort."

We streamed downward, faster and faster. It was at this point that the first serious doubts appeared in my mind — not about the elevator, of course, but about my fellow passenger. After all, he was only human. And he was looking decidedly ashen. When his knees began to buckle, I offered my arm for support. But my approach seemed to galvanize him and he sprang back up to his full height. The buzzer had faded, but there was a rattling noise that made him look upward and around, like the rear gunner in a Lancaster.

Somehow, I had to distract his attention. "Have you ever looked closely at the construction of a dental drill?" I ventured.

Although his breathing was as laboured as a CPR Hudson on full load, and his eyes were now bloodshot, I thought he could hear me. His tormented expression accused me of madness. The mere possibility disturbed me.

"No? Perhaps you don't see the connection. I mean to say that the wheels on new elevators are built by a company that used to make pulleys and what not for dental equipment. High-quality stuff. Far superior to the old wheels. They probably used them on this elevator, so you needn't worry on that score. Don't you find it fascinating that somebody could turn his attention from tiny parts for air-driven equipment to huge devices like elevators?"

Silence fell between us as I watched his hand knead the limp glove. It was being eviscerated through the index finger. I was forced to conclude, in the sight of this gruesome necropsy, that there was no point in speaking further. He was oblivious to me, to the glove, to the world. His own private Hell was upon him: eternal free fall in an elevator.

I had failed. Failed to convey to him the image of those almost unbreakable gleaming steel cables; failed to inspire in him an appreciation of that harmony of motor and sheaves, of cable and weights; failed to convince him that mankind's wealth of experience with elevators could be his, allowing him to face his present situation and, through the use of fact and logic, sweep aside his demon fears. Most upsetting, I had failed to open his heart to the innate attractions, the delights, the exhilaration of elevators.

"Oh, I have slipped the surly bonds of earth." Elevators summon to my mind's eye visions of twelve-foot silk scarves, castor oil, thick woollen socks, and biplanes. Even now, out of respect for my sweat-sodden companion, I tried to suppress a smile of elation as passages from the *Bandy Journals* tumbled joyously into memory. Elevators do that to me. Controlled flight; Leonardo, Bleriot, McCurdy...

I became aware of a straining and groaning; we were decelerating strongly. The cabin began to creak. The sound of my companion's stertorous breathing filled the small space, and now the sweat poured into his open mouth.

Then suddenly we were there. A bell sounded and the doors tripped open. My passenger sprang out of the elevator with the speed of a famished mongoose. He stood panting, resting his head against the cool marble of the lobby wall. I had to try one last time.

"I can help you overcome your fear. I can show you that riding elevators can be exciting."

His breathing stopped. At first he looked distant and uncomprehending, but then he giggled. The giggle rose to a laugh, then to a piercing falsetto peal. He began to dance about the lobby, skipping and cackling. His gloves and hat he threw into the fountain, and they were followed by a handful of change and some keys. As the security guard became suspicious and approached us, my erstwhile companion did a little jump, clicked his heels in mid-air, and then, still shrieking wildly, whooshed through the revolving doors into the night.

This story appeared originally in The Idler, No. 12, March & April, 1987, as "The Fall, Rise, and Fall of Elevators", and under the pseudonym Cam Stirling.

Sunset

The Little Restaurant's big-hearted welcome never looked so good, and the first half of our mugs of beer vanished as if flash-evaporated. The ramshackle little diner squatted lopsidedly behind us, and from the wooden deck on which our rustic table and chairs rested, we gazed out over a long stretch of brown-sugar-sand beach and down to the lake, which draped itself languidly over a piece of the planet, as though over a giant Belgian crepe griddle. Another mug of beer each, then we would be tucking into steaks, likely finishing just as the drama of a Lake Huron sunset played out.

We four were an unlikely crew. Dragged in from odd corners of the technical support group, or what was left of it, we had maybe six years' work experience among us. This was our third day working together, and we had been brought in to deal with a chronic detector problem that had suddenly gone acute. It was acute because it had forced production down to forty percent. Phones lit up in the office of the site production supervisor. The instructions were to get that fucking plant back to one hundred fucking percent by yesterday afternoon because we are drowning in fucking red ink. The imperious demand to get Harold Jackson onto the job brought the unwelcome response "Can't. He was made redundant last month." The order then became simply "Find somebody. Get that rust bucket back to full speed. Do it!" and the click resulting from the phone at the other end being slammed down emphasized eloquently that Head Office's command was not negotiable.

In fact, everyone knew that Head Office was at that very minute a virtual shitstorm of finger pointing and recrimination. The local production supervisor, Mr. Boyd, knew it, and he knew that the recently installed hard-driving managing director, Mr. Mann, was now running for cover. It had been Mann's idea to slash plant costs and push for higher production, the oft-pursued quest for bottom-line Nirvana combining "intelligent operation" and "rationalized management of raw materials", doing more while using less, and then trimming, refining, tucking, shaving — until an infinite amount of product is generated from zero resource.

A suntanned arm rose against the blue sky to attract a waiter as he crossed the patio. "Four more please."

Four days ago, I knew the other three only by sight. We had been hidden away in separate corners, doing intern-level work. Then Boyd had come through in a cloud of panic, fingering anyone whose work wasn't nailed to one of the many unforgiving critical paths. There was a twenty-minute briefing, we were shoehorned into an airless office and told to solve the problem ASAP. We looked at each other and established our bona fides quickly.

"Marlow. Queen's", I said. "Mathematical physics."

The others followed suit.

"Bracken. Saskatchewan. Electrical."

"Forest. McGill. Chemical."

"Natick. Dal. Mechanical."

Within two hours on our first day, hounded by our implacable problem, we had settled into a solid working routine. Two long days, involving everyone casting a blind eye at daily and weekly working-hour limits, had forged us into a team. Two pub meals, this one being the third, had added camaraderie. The occasional involuntary yawn and the grey smudges beneath our eyes were just the seal on our newfound brotherhood.

By noon on the first day, we had worked our way through the thick binder left with us by Boyd and set it aside. It contained more than ten years of partial fixes, false starts, and pointless technical musings, and we concluded that it was little better than a dense thicket of conceptual traps. We all recognized that this was now no longer a carefree lark for summer students. We were in the real world up to our necks. There was a problem, and it was now down to us to find a solution. It was scary. But it was also exciting. We looked at each other. This was the big one. We couldn't let it get away.

I remembered my favourite professor advising never to be afraid of a problem, always look it right in the eye. Once you knew what the core problem was, you were halfway there. We talked our way around and into the situation we faced, identified problem elements, jotted down several dozen ideas, then began playing with them like jigsaw pieces. The hazy skein of a picture began to appear.

"You know", said Natick at one point, "this plant has no right to be operating at all. It's way past any credible warranty date."

"That would be a good judgment for a more modern design", Bracken observed. "But just look at this brute. It really is rugged. They've pushed it well beyond its original operating limits, and it's hardly batted an eye. The guys who designed this knew in their gut what they were doing, and they certainly knew how to design their way past gaps in their knowledge."

Everyone nodded at that. We had seen components that were forty years old, components out of production for more than twenty years but built so sturdily that only a little maintenance and some coaxing was enough to keep them going just fine. Even just a few days of hands-on work had raised a solid respect in us for the plant and for the men (and it was quite certain that, unfairly, they were all men back then) who had designed and built it. Sure, there were people more than willing to scoff at the clunky relays, the over-designed equipment racks, the rock-solid analogue meters. But to us, that was about the same as scorning the eight-hundred-year-old village church because it wasn't a cathedral.

Our second round of beer arrived.

The breakthrough occurred for us on the second day, when Bracken suggested that we back away and look at the problem again. We did. An hour later, we had three alternative statements to the one we had been focussed on earlier. Two hours after that, a fourth alternative flared up.

We were supposed to quit by six that evening. By two the next morning, we had an outline solution. No matter which way we looked at it, it looked good.

"We need six hours sleep", I said. "We're too hazy right now."

We stumbled to our accommodations, a group of old, cramped, and smelly trailers parked on some waste ground to accommodate students who didn't have the wheels to go into town to decent rooms that they couldn't pay for anyhow.

Comparing notes later, we agreed that, despite our fatigue, despite having flopped hopefully onto our bunks, our minds had refused to shut down. It was the artesian spring of youthful energy. We had all drifted into a restless sleep at about five a.m. By seven thirty, within fifteen minutes of each other, we had arrived back at our working space. We had tidied up before leaving a few hours earlier, but even so the place resembled a wildly drifted landscape after a fierce paper blizzard. We looked at each other and grinned. At the stubble we all wore. At hair from which restless sleep had not been combed. At my sockless feet stuffed hurriedly into unmatched shoes. At Forest's shirt on which the upper buttonhole leaned out in search of its button, now rammed awkwardly into the next hole down.

There was a note on our desk from the production supervisor. *Please update me for 9 a.m. conf with HO.*

"I'll go and bring him up to date", I said. "You guys keep working."

Twenty minutes later I was back to brief them.

"It's a holding action at best", Natick said. "He'll be around again in less than an hour." Nods of agreement. No comment in response. There was no time for that. Our first simulations showed that the model we had developed the previous evening was holding. The rising tide of excitement was lifting all our boats.

We soon had enough information to start identifying the field changes needed. I had forced us to stop every half hour, look back over what we had done, convince ourselves that we remained error free and were still on solid ground.

The prize hung before us, shimmered, scintillated. Within our grasp was something that had eluded waves of seasoned staff for more than ten years. The four of us, full of Conradian inspiration and drive, were straining to the finish line. A couple of hours more and we would have it. The steel of a seeming unquenchable youth pulsed in our veins.

Just before ten o'clock, the production supervisor rushed in. His face was full of a hope that knows it is about to be dashed. Where so many experienced people before us had gone down to defeat, surely what we were producing would turn out to be the bitterest chimera.

"Where have we got?" he asked rather too urgently. "I'm getting calls from Head Office every half hour."

"We have a field-change work plan. We need to clear it with the system engineer. Then we bring the system down, make the changes, run some start-up tests, and if all is well we bring it back online."

"There's no time for that", Boyd said in a mixture of excitement and despair. "Walk me through it. I'll sign."

We looked at each other, shrugged, then led him over to the table.

The walkthrough took about twenty minutes, during which time he asked only a handful of questions.

"Shit!" he barked at length. "Nobody's ever even thought of doing this before. Will it work?"

"The calculations are all there", Bracken said. "We can't find anything wrong with them."

Boyd chewed his lower lip. "Is there any way we can do a reality check?"

"Sure there is", Bracken said. "We can do a mock-up in the lab, but that would take at least another day, probably two."

I began to worry that the lower lip might become detached.

"Okay", Boyd said in sudden decisiveness. "Let's do this." At that stage, he was a driven animal, hunters in close pursuit behind him, having run out of hiding places, and clutching at a last desperate hope. He could see his dream of an upcoming retirement and its blessed release bending from the strain, threatening to break at any time, and for his sake, I knew at that moment we needed to prevail.

We walked through the thing once more with him, he signed off, told us to start making the field changes, and left to bring Head Office up to date.

The short account from there is that we brought the system down, made the changes needed, did the six tests, and all four of us grinned ear to ear when they came off without even the whisper of a hitch.

"Call Boyd", I said to Bracken. "Tell him we're bringing the system back up and handing it over to the control room, and that they can start raising production any time after that."

A few minutes later, the extension in our cubbyhole rang. "It's Boyd", said Bracken. "Head Office wants him to take production to one hundred percent in one jump."

We looked at each other.

"Oh, for God's sake!" barked Natick. "Tell him to grow some balls and stick to the forty–seventy–one hundred plateaux in the plan. It'll take only another hour."

We heard no more and went back to documenting our calculations, the work plan, the production raise, and put in the requests needed for changes to drawings. We made annotations to the maintenance manual, to the design manual, and to the instructions to the operators. We wrote a long memo to the production supervisor, and then suddenly we were finished.

We looked at each other in happy exhaustion. At ten to six that evening, Boyd came in. He was smiling. It was the smile of someone who had cheated the hangman this time, the wan smile of a broken, defeated, dispirited man, hammered to a pulp of professional disillusionment by the Head Office sausage machine.

"Thanks guys. Thanks. Thanks…" He came to a halt in this monosyllabic blind canyon, and I thought he was about to break down. But he just looked from one to another of us, nodded silently a few times, then said "Go get yourselves something to eat and drink. You've done great work here, now go and relax." We made some silent self-deprecatory hand motions, nodded, and began collecting our few things.

"You want to order gentlemen?"

I looked up from an empty tank reverie, groped my way mentally back to the restaurant patio, and said, "Give us another minute."

The sun was now about fifteen degrees above the horizon, and I was starving. There was not a hint of breeze, the lake was a polished reflector, and a long, brilliant solar tongue licked across it toward us.

"I'm having the biggest strip loin on the menu", I said, and there were nods of agreement all round. Bracken fixed a gaze on me for a few seconds.

"You're pretty straight up, Marlow, for a studious guy", he said, still holding me in his gaze. "What do you think happened there today?"

"I like to read", I agreed, "but I don't know how you get from there to me being studious. I like flipping burgers too, but that doesn't make me a master chef."

"It's not a criticism", Bracken added quickly. "But I see what you read, and you read a lot. I've heard of quite a few of the books I see you with, but I've never cracked any of them. Maybe you can tell me about them sometime."

"Sure. But I don't know what that has to do with what happened today."

Bracken smiled. "Well, nothing of course. But I'm so tired that I decided just to let two thoughts out while I had my mouth open."

A communal smile at this odd exchange was broken by the return of the waiter. We ordered our steaks and each took another long drink of beer. I laid my head back against the chair and looked up into the sky.

"There was a week during my work for my master's thesis", I began, "when everything just clicked, came together. It ended up clean and tidy, and I really was pleased to see how surprised and proud my prof was." There was a long pause here while I savoured that feeling once again. "But today we took on the real world, and we rode it to a standstill, when all the guys before us, quite a few of them more than twice our age, ended up in the dust. We've probably had all the thanks we're going to get for it, but then those clowns at Head Office wouldn't know a good model, like the one we put together, if it sneaked up and bit them on the ass." I paused here, raised my glass, and added "we fly well together, gentlemen".

The sun was now about two diameters above the lake surface, and was becoming more reddened and oblate.

The end of the day today would be, for the four of us, just the end of a day, but a day when we had seen for the first time, metaphorically, the purple hills at dawn and smelled the aromatic scents of a distant and exotic land. We had touched the East. Boyd, or rather Mr. Boyd, since he deserved that respect, was limping home to a tawdry and uninspiring harbour, but might, even yet, miss the jetty and grind onto the rocks. He had sailed for years, but had never seen those hills, never smelled those scents, and now it was way too late for him. Even worse, the Head Office yahoos were play-acting the role of a skipper looking cool and displaying nerves of steel, were gripping the wheel in a pose of masterful control, but were reading the wrong charts and heading full speed toward lethal shoals. Worst of all, while they would send down everything and everyone with the ship, they would be first into the lifeboats.

Our steaks arrived, and I bit into mine eagerly. Even as the day ebbed, strength flowed back into me, wild, indomitable, youthful strength.

The lower limb of the sun's arc touched the horizon, and a long flare ignited the water surface, the flame shooting across to us. Tomorrow would be another day, our youth would rise again, perhaps strain to reach new heights.

In a few minutes, the sun slid past the horizon, winked, and vanished.

Goodbye, *Judea*. All you stand for salutes you.

"Sunset" is a modern day salute to Joseph Conrad's "Youth".

Gordie

"Forty dollars? Wow! Sure thing!"

Bob and I liked hanging around the place. Sam had started *Sam's Marina* only seven years earlier, but the place quickly took root and grew because Sam was a natural raconteur, a brilliant mechanic, and a happy workaholic. I think that he basically charmed boat owners to bring their problems to him, and they did, drifting in by the dozen, like birds fluttering down from trees to a newly replenished feeder.

Sam always had at least three or four outboards mounted in his test tank, sometimes as many as ten. He would start them up, or try to start them up, and then listen closely to the sounds they made, put his hand on the housing to check temperature or vibration, sometimes even sniff the exhaust. It would take only a few minutes for the problem a particular motor was struggling against to become clear to him. In a few minutes more, he would have a good idea whether the motor could be repaired, how long it would take, and how much it would cost. Sam said he had had more than one owner bring a motor in and say, "You want it? Take it! Damn thing craps out every two weeks. Bunch of junk!" Those motors would very soon be in gleaming good health, and would be sold at bargain prices to happy new owners and run for years without a hiccough.

What Sam wanted us to do was take a canoe down into Stumpland and retrieve a small dinghy that had drifted from one of the larger sailing boats and ended up way off among the stumps.

"Don't ask", Sam said, shaking his head in disbelief, when we wondered how it managed to get way down there. "Sure, I could do it myself, but it would take me at least forty-five minutes, and in that time here, I can earn a couple hundred dollars. So by taking my forty bucks you'd be doing me a big favour."

As a result, the mouth of this gift horse would remain scrupulously unexamined.

We left Sam's repair room and its line of roaring, coughing, sputtering outboards. In five minutes, the red canoe Sam let us use whenever we wanted was in the water and we were slicing down the river toward Stumpland.

Now Stumpland is just what it sounds like — a large expanse of what was once an extended flat shore area home to thick stands of pine, cedar, and the occasional larch, but now, it was just a region of submerged and partially submerged stumps. Years ago, before either of us was born, water level control on the entire waterway was instituted, and this resulted in the extended flat shore being flooded permanently. Prior to this flooding, crews of men had happily taken up the offer to clear-cut the trees. So this part of the river was now a forest graveyard, a place that had quickly attracted the expressive and somewhat ominous moniker "Stumpland". It was shallow, slimy, semi-stagnant, and very much off limits to any craft other than a canoe. Even in a canoe, it was possible, indeed very easy, for someone lacking experience to get wedged among a group of stumps that could seem suddenly to become almost like malicious living things, grumpy amputees from an enchanted forest, closing in and locking firmly in place any unwary explorer. Like Shackleton in the ice. If that happened, the only salvation was to free the canoe by climbing out of it into an unknown depth of weeds, mud, slime, and some quite large squirmy things that probably had very nasty teeth or beaks. We knew one intrepid explorer who had become thus entrapped, but it happened to him only once; you couldn't pay him enough ever to venture into Stumpland again.

Bob and I knew Stumpland quite well. More importantly, for any area in Stumpland that was not well known to us, we had a routine for poking and testing ahead of us to avoid this situation of being stranded, or "up the stump", an expression that would bring a good ear-boxing if uttered within hearing of our mothers. Even so, although we never had to expose our feet to the evils of those muddy depths, our canoe bore the graze marks of a number of near entrapments.

The day was glorious. The sun poured its golden favours generously onto our tanned arms and legs. As we moved downriver, a light breeze huffed capriciously into our faces from The Narrows about a mile further downstream. To us, The Narrows always had the trappings of Exotica, as though it was the gateway to Ophir, to the spice lands of the East, or to sandy beaches, palm trees, and hordes of tropical beauties, all more than eager to ravage uninitiated boys, then wash them all over and lay them down in a bed of rose petals. The river we were skimming along passed through the middle of our village, on its way to The Narrows. A large maple forest marched away to our right. Two dentists in the large neighbouring town were kept gainfully employed by this maple forest.

"I'm glad I live here", Bob said from the rear of the canoe.

"Why?"

"Look around. Look at what we've got."

And he was right. The panorama from our canoe was a strong, silent expression of drama and invitation: to our left, the limestone cliffs beamed an assurance of rough but loving paternal strength; to our right, the moraine swelling up from the abdominal plain promised comfort and protection of a softer, gentler kind. To the north of the village, the river first widened almost to a small lake, then narrowed to a confined course about half a mile long, held firmly in place by limestone cliffs on both sides. The water flowed quietly but quickly here, and one had to paddle like a madman to make headway. On the right, as one faced upstream, spring water trickled at several locations from the limestone rock face and collected in lovely natural woodland pools a few yards back from the river's edge, pools worthy of a Narcissus. Luscious watercress made its home here.

At the north end of this defile, the limestone cliffs fell away to wooded banks, and a bit further up there was a spot where the river rushed through a gap in a large granite outcropping. The flow here was too swift to paddle against, but there was a single-file path that began about two hundred yards south of this natural sluiceway. It was easy to land the canoe where that path began, pull it by its painter upstream, carry it the last fifty or so yards over the granite outcrop, and launch it in calm water upstream, where the river widened again. Then, the routine was to canoe further up this widened area, turn, and take a run at the slot in the granite outcrop. By the time the bow of the canoe dipped into the rushing water in the narrow passage, canoe and passengers would be flying. It took some skill to make it through without capsizing. Bob and I were generally considered the masters of this run.

But despite all these advantages, for the hell of it, I decided to throw some sand into Bob's gears.

"Well, yes, there are some good things, but what about all the other stuff?"

"What other stuff?" Bob bristled defensively.

"What other stuff? You're joking! What about the fact that we're the only village in the area that a convicted murderer came from? Or that our hockey team is the dirtiest in the bush league? Or that there are more drunks in our village than in any other in the region? Are you proud of all that?"

"No", Bob said in a pouty voice. "I just choose to ignore it. It's got nothing to do with me. I like to think about all the quirky but harmless things."

"Such as?"

"Well, like old Bobby who drags his wagon around the village every morning starting at six thirty, singing *Lily The Pink* and saying he's off to do some "haulage", even though there's never anything in the wagon. Like Simon who's almost forty now, couldn't make it past grade three, and has a whale of a time playing Kick the Can with the ten-year-olds. Like Morty who drives the village snow plough and has lost four sets of false teeth because he was unlucky enough, four times, to try spitting through the cab window just when the plough struck a curb. Like dotty Henry, the village eccentric, who spends his mornings all summer panning for gold in the river. Like Gordie."

Everybody knew about Gordie, a beautiful young boy, very friendly, the apple of everyone's eye, but very dim and not able to learn at all — spent three years in grade one, then was let off school by special dispensation.

"I never knew Gordie", I said.

"I didn't either."

"How come we all know about him?" I asked.

"Everybody just does", Bob said. "Like the lumber mill. Everyone calls it Jackson's Mill, but nobody seems to know anything about who Jackson was."

"Strange", I said. "I've never thought about it much before."

"My Mum said Gordie's family moved away", Bob said.

There were a few other odd stories that I could have added, like the madly puritanical Pentecostal minister who goes out early every Sunday morning behind the church in a fit of rage and disgust to harvest the fresh crop of used condoms from the night before. Like Helena, who, once she's had a few, uses her beautiful singing voice to fill the streets on Saturday night with the rich sound of opera arias but then branches off into any one of a number of dirty songs. But I thought that maybe things like that went somewhat beyond the definition of "quirky".

We paddled on. It was a "good mood" morning, in full swing. Stumpland was just a few hundred yards further now.

"Which way do you want to go in?" Bob asked. "Through the North Channel, Middle, Channel, or South Channel?" These were our safe routes into Stumpland.

"Let's see where the dinghy is first."

We cruised slowly along the edge of Stumpland, and after just a few minutes, we saw it — a small blue-and-white dinghy about sixty or seventy yards in, amid a thick copse of stumps.

"I think it's the Middle Channel", I said. Bob agreed, but added that we should go straight in as far as we could on the route we knew and try to see how the dinghy got where it was. "It probably will be easiest to take it out the way it went in."

That made sense to me, so we started in. We worked the canoe in about fifty yards. "This is as far as we've ever gone on the Middle Channel", I said. The dinghy was now sitting ahead and off to the left. I moved up to the very front of the canoe and scanned the way ahead. We had about a foot of water beneath us, and it looked like there was a path forward curving off toward where the dingy rested, and a sort of small lagoon about twenty yards further in, so we slowly manoeuvred the canoe forward.

Twice we had to back up because we were stopped by something underneath — an impassable barrier of stumps or discarded bits of tree trunk. Eventually, we made it past a final clump of stumps and into the lagoon, which was smaller than it looked, and we could hear the bottom of the canoe scraping over branches or snags. It was very swampy here, and the canoe and our paddles were stirring up some pretty odorous muck, but it did look as though this was how the dinghy might have drifted in.

We turned the canoe to the left and began moving ourselves toward the dinghy. An exclamation from Bob made me turn my head. His nose was wrinkled, and then I smelled it too. It was vile.

"What the hell is that?" I asked.

"Don't know", Bob said, sounding like he was trying not to woof. "Looks like an old bag of garbage."

"Where?"

Bob pointed with his paddle. "I can't... I've never...", he mumbled through his nausea.

"It's yellow . . . I've never seen any garbage bag like that."

"Come on", Bob said unsteadily, trying to hold down his breakfast. "Let's get the dinghy and get out of here."

That sounded like a good plan. We made our way to the dinghy, tied its painter to the rearmost strut in the canoe, and started working our way back toward the river. As we moved back past the garbage bag, about ten yards away in a bed of weeds, I took one final look. Odd shape. Smooth. Big lumps protruding from it. Then we were back in the Middle Channel and, five minutes later, out in the river.

We delivered the dinghy to Sam, collected our forty dollars, then hung around the shop for a while. We watched Sam diagnose a few more sick outboards, make notes on each, and stick these instructions for the mechanics onto the housings of the motors.

"Did you know Gordie?" I asked Sam.

Sam stopped, turned and looked at Bob and me. "Ye-es. What makes you ask about Gordie?"

"We were just thinking about all the quirky people in the village when we went off to get the dinghy, and Gordie's name came up. Neither of us ever met him, and we just realized that it's odd we should know about someone we never met."

"There's not much to tell. He was a very good-looking, very sweet young fellow. Spent time over there" — Sam pointed toward the other side of the river — "sitting on the dock fishing. He was quiet, but when anyone said hello to him, he would always smile, walk over, and say hello back. Everyone loved him. Secretly, we all felt sorry for his father. His mother was sent away to hospital not too long after Gordie was born."

We watched Sam work for a while longer.

"They moved away, didn't they?" Bob asked.

"Well, Gordie's father and sister moved away."

"What about Gordie?" I asked.

Sam looked at us steadily for a moment. "I guess you're old enough for me to tell you." But then he just stood there, looking into the distance, searching for the right words.

"Nobody is really certain. Jimmy Bingham was the only one who saw anything, but he was only five, so it's hard to be sure … but he said that Gordie just jumped in. Right off the bridge. Head first. Just like Ronnie Reynolds. Nobody really believed Jimmy, thought he probably made it all up. Ronnie Reynolds used to show off doing swan dives off the upper railing of the bridge into the river."

There was a long pause. "So what happened?" Bob asked.

"Nothing. Gordie never returned home that day. They searched everywhere. Thought he probably wandered off someplace, got lost, couldn't find his way home, and well … the police said they doubted that he jumped in the river, or fell in, because they never found a body."

"Sam", I said, as an unpleasant cold feeling spread across my abdomen. I swallowed from a dry mouth and looked at Bob, who was wide-eyed and pale.

The garbage bag.

"I think we just found Gordie."

A Bringer of New Things

The dog always looked up at him, seeming to ask "What now?"

"What now indeed, my old friend?"

They looked at each other, the dog blinked, began wagging his tail after ten seconds or so, hesitantly at first, then with enthusiasm. The man smiled, then burst out laughing, and the dog placed his front paws on the man's legs, tail waving furiously. There was happy barking and some skirmishing around the kitchen, then the man dug into the familiar red plastic container and gave the dog a small handful of treats.

"We have to go out for our morning walk, pick up a newspaper on the way back, and do a bit of shopping. Then we can have breakfast — you'd like that wouldn't you — yes, I thought so. Then I have some letters to write, I want to go and see if William needs anything, and after that we can go and have coffee with Andrew. By then it will be just about time for lunch. And this afternoon! Well, there's a lot to do! We'll take my sketchbook to the park. You'd like that, wouldn't you? Then I have to prepare for my book club meeting, I should spend an hour on my Spanish, and at four o'clock Henrietta is dropping in for tea and some cake, so I need to make the cake. We've got a full day ahead, Bruce my boy."

The sight of the leash being taken from its hook in the closet sent the dog skittering to the door where he stood whining impatiently and wondering why it was taking so long to clip the lead onto his collar. But then they were ready, the door was opened, they stepped out onto the porch, and the man locked up behind them.

"Morning, Sandy! Morning, Bruce!" This greeting came from the next-door neighbour, who was out weeding his flower beds.

"Good morning, Doug. Looks like a fine day ahead."

"The best, Sandy. Should top twenty-five degrees today."

The two men waved, and Sandy and Bruce set off down the street. The sun was already warm on their faces, and the trees and hedges were brimming in sparrows. Three people waved at Sandy from a distance, and two women stopped to say hello to Bruce and ask Sandy how he was doing. Bruce found yet another interesting lamppost, but his supply of holy water had run out, and a few drops was all he could manage. Their walk continued. After about forty minutes, they reached a small corner shop run by Amir, and Sandy picked up his daily newspaper. The return journey followed a different route, passing William's house, where Sandy checked that his older friend was all right and didn't need anything, after which they carried on for a hundred metres or so to a smallish supermarket where Sandy bought some milk, eggs, stewing meat, broccoli, and two custard tarts.

Bruce knew when he was in the home stretch, and like Sandy, he was far more interested in moving on to the next adventure than dragging out the present one. The dog was beginning to strain against the leash, wanting the pace to be a bit more brisk.

"Patience, Bruce. Patience. It's a beautiful morning, and the rest of our day will come along soon enough."

At length, man and dog returned home, the newspaper was placed on the table, the food just purchased was arranged in the fridge, and Sandy put down some food for Bruce then got out bread and bacon for his own breakfast. Bruce finished his meal, had a long drink from his water bowl, then went to lie on his mat and watch Sandy. Sandy also got out what he needed for the lemon cake he would make. As he moved back and forth across the kitchen, he passed the red cupboard repeatedly, and each time he did so, Bruce's ears perked up only to slump again when the distinctive doggy treats container failed to appear.

Sandy found that cooking had its own internal charms, mysteries, and attractions. It was not just the act of creating something. Sandy was curious about everything, and somehow that made even the most frequently repeated activities new and different.

His bacon was sizzling and ready, and his toast popped just as he completed measuring out the dry ingredients for the cake. Toast buttered and bacon tamped dry in paper towel, Sandy moved to his kitchen table, and without having to be invited, Bruce rose from his mat and lay down next to his master's chair. Outside the window, not six feet away, a small gang of goldfinches was squabbling over the niger seed in the feeder. Sandy watched birds throughout the year, being careful to switch to different seed as the bird populations shifted. He spent a few minutes thinking about their lives, the various risks they ran, the huge distances they had to cover, the few seasons they had to reproduce, and despite all that, the energy they seemed to bring to everything.

Bruce had his breakfast treat, a small end of bacon. Sandy placed the dirty dishes in the sink, finished preparing the cake batter, poured it into the tin, shoved it into the oven, which was now at temperature, and set the timer. While the cake was baking, he looked through the paper quickly, finding the articles he would spend time on later, having his usual crack at the crossword, and getting out notepaper and pen to write the two letters he wanted to mail that afternoon. These letters were replies to notes he had received three days ago, one from an old university friend with whom he had reconnected only a couple of years earlier, and the other from his sister-in-law in Charlottetown, a lovely little city he very much wanted to visit again. In the same post, he had received the annual flyer for the coming year's continuing education courses at Ryerson, and he groaned once more at how many appealed to him and at how much he would love to dig into the details of so many topics.

He finished his letters just in time to remove the cake from the oven, turn it out from its pan onto a rack, and set it aside to cool. Later, lunch would be a salad, which would take him only a few minutes to make, but just now he realized that he had to get moving in order to make his appointment with Andrew.

It had been almost a year since Andrew's arthritis began preventing him from walking to the local coffee shop, La Cafetière, but Andrew's beautiful back garden was even better. He had fruit trees and a long vegetable garden raised sufficiently that he didn't need to bend down too much to work on it, but most importantly, Andrew had a large outdoor patio that included a picnic table and comfortable chairs arranged beneath a canopy of vines.

Bruce went through the "Oh, goody! We're going for a walk!" routine once more, and they set out for Andrew's house. Twenty minutes later, Sandy was seated with Andrew on the patio, coffee before them, Scottish shortbread on a plate to one side, and Bruce lying beneath the table — and pretty much everything was right in their world.

"How are you today, Andrew?"

"Fine thanks. The warmer weather makes it a lot easier for me to move around."

Andrew was retired and had left his profession behind completely.

"Accountants are boring", he had said many times during his first year of retirement. "There must be a boring gene, and somehow accountants have managed pretty much to corner it exclusively for themselves."

"Maybe the interesting accountants just leave and do something else."

"Or maybe they just jump off a bridge", Andrew said drily.

"You're not boring."

"No", Andrew said, equally drily. "Not now. But I was inoculated after I retired."

Sandy let this one go because he knew that pursuing it would mean a forty-five minute lecture on the ability of Dante's *Divine Comedy* to give one a balanced personality and a healthy outlook on life. Over the past three years, Andrew had become something of a minor expert on that classic work of literature, could recite large chunks of it, and would embark on just such a recitation given the least encouragement.

They had their coffee and talked about all sorts of things, sitting under the vine leaves, enjoying the light breeze and the warm air.

An hour later, they shook hands, and then Sandy and Bruce left. Sandy had brought his sketchbook with him, and they took the long way home, through the park, down into the ravine, and along the lakeshore. The ravine was cool and quiet, and Sandy stopped twice, first to sketch a little-used path as it meandered up the steep slope of the ravine and second to do a detailed drawing of a small maple sapling that had grown perfect, unblemished leaves. Sketching really was therapy, of that Sandy was convinced, as was the regular round of meeting his friends.

All this was a clear sign, at least as far as Sandy was concerned. Over the years, the great variety of the world had impressed itself upon him, a variety that was, in effect, infinite. Just to be alive — to be faced by all the things that one could do, the people one could meet, the enjoyment one could derive in these people's company, and what one could learn from them — these were things that brought such exquisite feelings of connection and peace. This was so precious, and it was something he would need to try, once again, to put into words when he got home. Even as he thought this, lines he had learned in school tumbled into consciousness, he hoped correctly: "Every hour is a bringer of new things."

And that's about right, Sandy thought.

"Never mind this tattered coat upon a stick business. We're made of different stuff, hey Bruce?" And he made to carry on down the street but the dog just looked at him.

Sandy shook his head. "You're right. I'm a silly old bugger", he muttered to himself. He looked at the dog, who looked back expectantly, wagged his tail uncertainly, still immobile, looking up at Sandy. He smiled at the dog.

"Okay Bruce. Let's go then", and they moved on.

Looking forward, looking ahead. Still plenty to do.

A General Drama of Pain

The dog always looked up at him, seeming to ask, "What now?"

"What now?" the man said back to the dog. *Damn good question.* It was just another day. Another day that he had to fill. Somehow.

There was bright sunlight shining in through the window. There were the usual morning things — shaving, having toast and coffee, feeding Jimmy — but then what?

Well, Jimmy would need to go for a walk. He had tried picking different dog walking routes for a while, but it all became something of a pointless exercise, since Jimmy didn't seem to care. So now he just followed the same route every day.

On more than one occasion, he had met Sandy and Bruce. Sandy had been friendly, tried to engage him in conversation. But what was there to talk about? Really. There had evidently been things in Sandy's life that had left him happy. He had no idea what those things were, but they certainly hadn't made an appearance in his own life. There were years of boring work, work mates he seemed to have nothing in common with, temperamental bosses, and then being chucked in the trash can a year before his expected retirement date.

He had enough money. Enough money! *Enough for what, exactly?* He had a brother who phoned regularly, but only to ask for a handout. There were a few acquaintances he had an occasional drink with, but the only things they talked about were the weather and hockey. That filled one evening a week. Big deal!

He had been married for twelve years, and then, mostly out of mutual exhaustion and facing a massive wall of indifference, they had agreed to go their own ways. The people in the bank and the supermarket were friendly, and they expressed their muted sadness to learn that he and his wife had separated. They were nice people, but he had to face it, apart from helping him with his banking and selling him his groceries, they were strangers.

For about three years, he had tried going to public lectures. But he found that discussions of heritage properties were too earnest, and let's be honest about it, a losing battle. Discussions of current novels didn't do it for him. And lectures on Type II supernovae were just, well … remote, irrelevant, incomprehensible.

He had Jimmy. But at twelve years old, Jimmy was now going stiff and a bit lame. He was a friendly dog, but when the man looked into Jimmy's eyes, they were large, black, liquid, and full of what really seemed to be an insuperable sadness.

No. It was more than just sadness. It was that distant, leaden, low-level pain that no pain killer can remedy, the pain of isolation — meaninglessness, purposelessness, being beyond the reach of any joy. He had come to terms with it, sort of, a long time ago. He always had an inkling where it might lead.

He roused himself somewhat at the thought of a nice salad for lunch, and he would give Jimmy his favourite food, since he liked the way Jimmy recognized the tin, wagged his tail, ate with as much gusto as an old dog could muster, and then fell asleep almost immediately by his feet, next to the big grey armchair. When he had made it, the salad looked very appetizing indeed and tasted just as good. He ate it slowly, enjoying every bite, knowing that, like all things, he would finish it, it would come to an end all too soon, then he would be tossed back into the waiting-for-the-next-thing-to-happen queue.

For some reason, he thought of *The Mayor of Casterbridge*, but just as quickly dismissed the thought as one of those irrelevant neural flares.

Jimmy ate his meal, but when he went to take a drink of water, he slopped a great deal and seemed to be shaking his head. He whined, walked around the kitchen in a ragged circle, something that wasn't usual at all, then lay down and whimpered. This was worrying. Jimmy was his friend.

The day had turned dark, but it probably would not rain. Low clouds ran before an impatient and unfriendly wind. He thought he might doze in his chair, but then wondered what he would do later.

The prospect of an empty, metronomic day stretched out before him. He didn't want to think about it, but he found that there really was nothing else to think about.

It was time to take Jimmy for a walk. The dog's tail wagged uncertainly at the sight of the leash, and the man thought maybe he would abandon the plan, but then decided that was what they would do, what they had to do.

Today.

He went to the cupboard to get the dog's lead, then paused. He returned and sat at his kitchen table and wrote for ten minutes — a note. Then he rose, he and Jimmy left, and he locked the house after them.

The wind was gusting. The day was not welcoming. They walked slowly through several streets, then headed into the woods that covered high ground about half a mile from his house. The path was well worn, the trees at least broke the wind, and because of the weather, they had the place to themselves. They climbed through the trees to a high open meadow, and he walked Jimmy to the other side where thick bushes hid a rocky outcrop. They sat down on one of these large stones, and he pulled out a small bowl and a bottle of water and poured some for Jimmy. The dog drank.

Then the man held out his hand. "Here you are, Jimmy", he said, and the dog crunched the few treats, then lay down panting lightly.

The man swallowed a few of the treats himself, then lay back on the stone.

Thinking about the note on his kitchen table, he said "It won't be long now Jimmy."

The dog's ears pricked at the sound of his name, his breathing slowed briefly, expectantly, then he began panting once more, waiting for the next bit of excitement.

"So long, Jimmy."

The Crystal Path Home

The air was sparkling, and a word from early in his French studies came back, a word that he always loved: *étincelant*. It looked as though the air was filled by tiny snow or ice crystals — delicate points of sapphire, emerald, ruby, and flashing indigo diamond danced all around. It was crystalline happiness being scattered gently through an indefinitely large volume of space.

Giant snowflakes and large stylized icicles — smooth, regular, light bounding round inside them in diamond purity — seemed to wheel in the air. An object slowly turned in space, a tetragon, flashing light from its faces and edges, inexpressibly beautiful. The other regular solids floated by, the light coming from them was increasingly more extravagant, more nuanced: the stately cube, the elegant octahedron, the inviting dodecahedron, the sublime icosahedron. He watched them turn and flash in a subtle drama of movement and light. He wanted them to stay and perform forever. They were old friends revealing new sides, but they drifted off.

Now a new performance began, more complex, more figurative, and much more powerful. Shapes turned and wheeled, as if in a mist, and then in a shock of excitement, the thirty-two crystal classes moved in complex unison across a vast stage before him. They turned, transmitted telepathically their symmetry and supreme elegance, each one moving forward as if to take a valedictory bow. He willed them to continue, not to leave, but they too took their graceful symbolic farewells and faded.

Another act started, basic but gradually displaying more structure, more content, more complexity. He was entranced, but still he looked for understanding, for something to be revealed. And then it was there.

His mind suddenly encompassed it, something he had never done before, and the intellectual stimulation seemed unfathomable, incomprehensible, almost too beautiful and too extravagant to bear. In the distance, through a diaphanous, glowing mist, there was something, a massive reality, a vast entity whose symmetry was at once both blindingly evident and beyond reach. It pulsed, partly perceived, as if behind a thin silk veil, portions of it surged forward, then retreated. There was a number, not a large number in the scheme of things, but in the context of the reality he was witnessing, it was massive, stupendous, floating just beyond reach as a physical essence. And yet he knew it.

There was light everywhere. He was now one with the vast entity, the massive reality. Excitement, anticipation, happiness, they all tingled through his being. Yes! There was a unity! Yes! There was a purpose! Yes! He was becoming part of it all! It was ineffable. It was more sublime that he could ever have imagined. It was … it was … it was …

The light was subdued, and although not harsh, it was characterless against the reflective smooth floors and the institutional cream walls.

They looked down at the bed.

"I'm sorry. We did everything we could."

The woman was marked by life, grief, and acceptance. Her thick white hair and strong features bore that particular elegance of age. "I know. Thank you, doctor."

The doctor hesitated. "A personal note, if I may."

She nodded.

"I was fortunate enough to study from one of his minor texts on crystallography at university. He was a true professor, a genuine teacher. I looked at that text just a few days ago, and I was struck again by its clarity and elegance. Although I didn't know him personally, still I feel I owe him a great debt."

"Thank you", she said through a faint smile.

She looked down at him, brushed a hand gently through his thin white hair. "Did he suffer?"

"No, I don't believe he suffered. I did get the sense, more than once" — the doctor looked down at his hands — "I did get the sense that he experienced considerable joy."

They looked at one another and they knew...

"The Crystal Path Home" was inspired by concepts described so admirably in Mark Ronan's excellent little book *"Symmetry and the Monster"*.

Forty

"Yet another breathtaking dawn", James murmured dully to himself. He rubbed eyes that he knew were red and puffy, rasped a hand over the stubble on his cheeks and chin, and wondered why it all had to be this way.

So, here he was, at six in the morning, sitting in his comfortable and well-appointed condo, moping. He had watched as the sun, still concealed, set the eastern horizon smouldering, and only a few minutes ago, roar its red-hot entry into another day. The Don River pumped a lethargic column of clay- and silt-laden water out into the lake. And then there was Lake Ontario itself, that vast, inspiring inland sea that was simply ignored by most people who lived near it.

He rose from his leather sofa, where he had spent the night ruminating, walked to the bathroom, and splashed cold water over his face.

The mental refrain "time to take stock" drifted across his consciousness, but each repeat inventory of his life was now like a tongue returning endlessly to one chipped tooth among thirty-one other perfect specimens. During the night, he had reviewed that inventory yet again, looking for the unexplored corner, the unrecognized rough diamond, the concealed pathway yet to be followed. It had come out the same, as always, and the elements of his life were queued up before his mind's eye, the same shelf of pointlessly dutiful toy soldiers.

He could still remember the excitement awakening in the face of his teacher when James, then six years old, listened to the teacher's question, then calmly began writing out the terms for the correct infinite converging series. That same day, at lunch time, his teacher had shown him a plastic model of the conic sections and taken about ten minutes explaining the algebraic expression for a circle. James had studied the plastic model intently for ten minutes and, after three tries, produced the correct algebraic expression for an ellipse. He then looked at the model again, his eyes lit up, and he wrote out the expression for the parabola, which he referred to as an "almost ellipse".

By the age of ten, he knew clearly that, shown a physical situation, he could see — could read — the mathematical expression describing it, and he knew what was meant physically by an algebraic expression presented to him in isolation. The symbols spoke to him.

Nobody paid all that much attention to James' fascination at the trumpet music of Leroy Anderson. It was considered one of those passing boyish enthusiasms. But one teacher took note and asked him about it. James said that it was the pure sounds. The teacher had asked about piano music, but James just shook his head uncomprehendingly. The teacher then led James to the piano, struck some chords, played some arpeggios, noticed James sudden focus, then opened a music book to "Für Elise" and began to play. Another teacher who was nearby moved over to watch and later said she noticed that James' eyes didn't leave the sheet music. There was some discussion of the notes, the primacy of Middle C and where Middle C was on the sheet. James reached across in front of the seated teacher and tried to place his hands on the keys. The teacher shifted to one side on the bench, James sat before the keyboard, focussed intently on the page in front of him, then slowly played a rough version of the right hand of "Für Elise". The timings were wrong, but the two teachers were slack-jawed in astonishment.

Thus began James' meteoric climbs in mathematics and music.

James' adolescence was one explosion after another of beauty, revelation, insight, and discovery. By the age of eleven, he had mastered the standard works on calculus. At thirteen, he was deep into differential equations and had discovered, on his own, the integrating factor method. At fifteen, group theory was his obsession, and he had anticipated the elements of Lie groups before ever opening a text on the topic. His advance through piano music was similarly dizzying. At ten, he was enthralled by the music of Franz Liszt. At twelve, he had whistled through "The Well-Tempered Clavier" and had discovered the music of André Mathieu. At thirteen, he made his first formal concert appearance, and at fifteen, he cut his first full-length recording.

At the age of sixteen, James collapsed.

The doctors called it complete nervous exhaustion, and he had six months of enforced, total rest.

It was hell.

James' later adolescence and on into his early twenties was a surging, delirious, magical, febrile ascent. In ninety frenetic hours a week, he devoured mathematics at university and blew everyone away when he expanded an off-hand comment by Grothendieck into a hundred-and-thirty-page opus. That work was the basis for a swift passage through the PhD requirements. By the age of twenty-seven, James had published eighteen highly original mathematical papers and made ten recordings, but then the fountain began to run dry. Cruelly, someone sent him a copy of "A Mathematician's Apology". He agreed to give several popular concerts, but he disliked the experience greatly and declined all further requests.

So ... here I am. The sun had pulled the blanket of night from the sky, and the new day had struggled to its feet. In a few minutes, James would undertake his daily forty-five-minute fast walk along the lakeshore. Maybe today the fresh air would make a difference, maybe some inspiration would rise within him, indicating some formula, some path, some means for breaking free from this condition of stasis, of angst, of entrapment.

"Let's not go there again", James thought. "I don't need a close examination of my condition. I know it. It is derailment, disillusionment, disappointment. Descent." He knew it well.

Descent — that was certainly the apt word. He felt he was in a slow descent, from what had been the height of his physical and mental powers at the age of thirty-two. From a sun-kissed region where his orientation was one of hopeful striving and aspiration. What had once been a tingling sense of imminent arrival had given way to a feeling of wandering in foggy lowlands bereft of any worthy destination.

Of course, he had received advice.

You've always tried to do way too much.

You've accomplished more in your time than most could manage in ten lives.

An extended holiday, a change of pace and scene...
I know a specialist...
Maybe you should just try growing up, James.

James' ominous "ship in the night" would soon emerge from the mist and vanish into it again just as quickly.

His fortieth birthday.

He had agreed, reluctantly, to a small celebration. He knew how it would go. There would be lifelong friends — true friends — but even so, it would be a strain.

And on that day, he would cross a portal — one through which no traveller is ever handed a coveted Fields Medal. Becoming a companion of René Thom, Michael Atiyah, Alain Connes, Edward Witten, Timothy Gowers, and others would then pass from being a trembling hope to a shattered dream.

To take some kind of solace and to ponder a musical figure whose misfortune had been far worse than his own, James put on Mozart's great Symphony No. 40 in G minor. He had read the many commentaries of it. Ringing phrases, to be sure — he rejected them all, but he knew what Wolfgang had meant. James had applied the full musicological apparatus to the 40th, had studied it minutely, knew every note of it. Now it soared again through space and time, spoke to him in a way that nothing else in the body of classical work could do.

The sun was rising in the sky. Time. It had always been something he needed to watch. Tight schedules. Days always full. That had fallen away. But he still did have things booked. Like his meeting today. His heart wasn't in it, but it had been arranged weeks earlier. Dressed informally, he set out reluctantly and without expectations. He had pulled together some elementary written material on mathematics and on music. And he tried to keep an open mind.

As he met the students, James recalled the request that had brought him to this school. *Please talk to us about music.* Impossible to interpret, seen from an adult perspective. James wondered once more about why he had agreed to come. But he was here now. He looked around the room. There were about twenty youngsters, all of them around five or six years old, and a half dozen staff, attendants, including the man who had arranged on an earlier occasion for James to play the piano and speak to a group of older children at the same institution.

But this ... this was very different. *I'll stay for a couple of hours, then that will be the end of it.*

He talked to the children as a group, then moved among them to answer any questions, of which there were few. Until he came to one of them. A boy who quite clearly had limited capacities. The boy looked at James innocently.

"My name's Alastair."

James didn't know what to say.

"Are you here to teach us?"

"Well, yes... I can", James said, caught off balance initially. "Is there something you'd like to learn?"

"I don't know." Alastair looked at James in open curiosity. "Are you a teacher?"

"Well, no ... but I can teach."

Alastair looked puzzled. "What do you do?"

Good question, James said to himself.

"Well, I play the piano. And I like problems."

Alastair was now more relaxed. A fleeting smile crossed his features.

"Problems?"

"Yes. Like these." And James reached for one of the file folders he had brought with him. He opened it and turned so that Alastair could see the diagrams.

"What are they?"

"Well, this is geometry, but I also have—"

James looked at Alastair who was now climbing up onto his lap. Alastair smiled up at James, and then began turning pages in the file that was open in front of him. The boy was concentrating, and his face beamed out that fact.

A colourful diagram showing Pythagoras' Theorem was on the page before them. Alastair pointed toward it.

"That's a funny looking building."

James smiled, told Alastair it wasn't a building, then reached for another folder. "How about this one?" he asked Alastair. They flipped through the first few pages.

"What is it?"

"Well, it's arithmetic."

"What do you do with it?"

"Oh! You can do all sorts of things with it. Here. I'll show you." But having said that, he wasn't sure where to go from there.

James looked around. On a table a couple of metres away was an assortment of colourfully painted small wooden cubes.

"Let's get those blocks", James said. "I'll show you."

He set Alastair down on the floor, walked with him over to the table, and picked up as many of the blocks as he could carry in two hands.

"Are we going to play?"

"Yes", James said. "Let's play", and he looked around. "Let's play right here on the floor."

James dropped the blocks on the floor, they clattered and bounced around, and Alastair laughed.

"We're not supposed to throw our toys on the floor."

James looked around. He leaned toward Alastair. "I don't think anybody noticed", he whispered. Alastair laughed again.

Soon they were both lying on their stomachs on the floor. James placed two blocks together, then three blocks together but about a foot away, then another set of five blocks further away. He moved the blocks around, telling Alastair what he was doing.

Suddenly Alastair's face lit up, and he laughed again.

"Let's do another one!"

And they did. And another after that. And another and another. Alastair's laughter echoed around the room and James noticed the expression of surprise on the face of one of the attendants.

James pulled a sheet of music from another folder and placed it on the floor in front of Alastair. He pointed at the notes and looked at Alastair.

"Is that arithmic too?"

"No. It's music."

"Is it…? Can we use the blocks?"

"No. It's a set of instructions. Here's what they mean", James said, and as he moved his finger from note to note on the sheet, he sang "Da da da da da da da da dahhhh, da da da dahhhh, da da da dahhhh", sounding out the first bars of Für Elise.

"Now you try it."

"No", Alastair laughed. "I can't."

"Sure you can", James said. "Let's do it together."

And they did. Their voices blended: "da da da da…"

Alastair laughed joyously.

By this time, several of the staff had gathered round. They were smiling. But also, James thought, they were surprised.

James pulled out more pieces of music. He led Alastair through the notes. Alastair laughed and smiled in pleasure. They sang and talked and played with the blocks. All afternoon. It was the light in Alastair's eyes…

That evening, in a state of surprise, confusion, and delight, James spent three hours thinking about the coloured blocks and the sheets of music. He made notes. On arithmetic and on music.

For Alastair.

For the boy he really knew nothing about. The boy who had smiled innocently and touched James' face. The boy who wanted his help. The boy he laughed with. The boy who trusted him.

That same evening, James planned what he was sure would be his new life.

Little Brother

The weather had been mixed but was mostly fine and warm. Large cumulus clouds were passing overhead just now, but the haze and the grey horizon to the south indicated that something different was on the way.

The bicycle path was good and well marked, and surprisingly, there were few other people out. Maybe they knew something about the weather that I didn't. The breeze was typical of summer, gusty and capricious. Wooded hilltops made the landscape distinctive, somehow reassuring. A couple of hawks cruised languidly, probably just as a way to pass a summer day, but still keeping an eye out for any midmorning snack. I cycled on at a steady pace, enjoying not just the superb bike path but the whole package of weather, scenery, fresh air. I had done this route before and knew which villages were worth a short detour, where the good places were to stop for a rest or for lunch.

Generally familiar features and landscape drifted past. Apart from the very attractive towns and villages, there were a few things I looked forward to in particular. And around the next long bend, I knew what to expect — yet their sudden appearance always seemed to surprise me: the Twelve Apostles — large limestone promontories, jutting out from the steep wall that defined one side of the Altmühl valley. After a long stop, standing astride my bike just to gaze at them, I started out again, advancing slowly and watching each of the Apostles as they drifted past.

Do they have names? Is this large imposing one Simon? That one, two further along, is that Andrew? And the one that seemed to be staring doubtfully at the river, is that Thomas? And that one there, now crumbled and blackened, is that Judas?

The last of them swept past me, and about fifteen minutes later, I entered a small village, the name of which I can no longer recall. A heat haze had now spread over half the sky, the sun had become a fuzzy orb, and it seemed to be saying to me "Sorry bub, you're about to get wet", even as I felt a first few drops of rain. It was about then that a church, not small and not large, but seeming somehow awkward and out of proportion, appeared on the right. *Any port*, I thought and parked and locked my bicycle to one side of the building. Bunches of weeds smirked blasphemously as they leaned in seeming casual impudent challenge against the church wall, which looked to be crumbling somewhat. The church, too large for the space it occupied, probably much loved and jammed full of worshippers at one time and looking as though it could have been — had wanted to be — a much larger building, was now sliding sadly into disuse. But at least it was a place out of the rain.

The door resisted my initial shove but then groaned and opened, and soon I was inside. The refreshing coolness, the relaxing darkness, and the peace — possibly a peace approaching terminal for this building — all combined to offer a modest but gracious welcome. The windows were small and mostly clear glass, though fitted parsimoniously with a little coloured glass, and were mostly opaque, cataractic, dimmed by layers of dust. The interior of the church beckoned me stoically, a lonely old lady, unaccustomed to visitors, but now sparingly applying some of her remaining makeup to express her delight at receiving an unexpected guest. Two votive candles burned contemplatively. A mild rumble signalled the fact that somewhere outside, but some distance away, a storm was passing.

Walking about halfway down the central aisle, I took a seat in one of the pews, laid my cycling helmet on the bench beside me, and began to take a closer look around, but then realized that I was not alone. Someone was shuffling paper.

The sound startled me, but almost instantly I recognized the opening bars of Gigout's Toccata in B minor. The organ was not a large one; I could see a couple of banks of pipes, and then I spotted the curly grey hair of the organist, waving and bobbing to the music he was making. After a short delay at the end of the Gigout piece, Robert Schumann's Opus 56 No. 3 sounded. A group of pieces by

Bach followed. There was the finale from Vierne's Symphony No. 1 for organ, a couple of pieces I didn't recognize, and then, just for fun, Widor's Toccata.

My damp and somewhat smelly cycling gear didn't matter, because I wasn't really in the little church anymore. It had spoken to its bigger brothers, and I was now transported to Salisbury, could see the graceful soaring spire, hear that cathedral's majestic organ. Then somehow, I was in York Minster, where the musical phrases from a Joseph Jongen concert spooled once more in my mind's ear. Cologne Cathedral, der Kölner Dom, rose up again before me, then the tumblers of time and geography rolled once more and the great organ and distinctive reverb from Notre Dame spoke to me from my past. I barely had time to glance at the great rose window when I recalled another evening and a concert from years earlier in Modena Cathedral, overlain by Pavarotti's rich tenor.

A long chord ended. The little church held and savoured the dying echo for as long as it could. The organist stood, waved to me, and then was gone. I looked around the church. It wasn't the same place. I could still hear, feel, the music. Once again, in this unexpected setting, I was struck by the genius, honed over centuries, of dimension, volume, zinc tube, and composer, which could produce these great, aurally-led, sensory trips. The little church grew lighter as sun broke through the haze outside and smiled in through the windows.

Looking around again, but this time more slowly, more carefully, and not so arrogantly dismissive, I nodded.

Not bad. Not bad at all, Little Brother.

Sheldon

Sheldon could not remember a time when he was not Sheldon. And he could not remember a time when the boy was not there.

He smelled the wood shavings that lined his little box from the Humane Society shelter. The shavings stuck to him and he had to shake them off. He realized that he was hungry, and he stepped unsteadily out of the little box, wobbled on uncertain kittenish legs from beneath a table in the corner of the room, and immediately was seized in alarm as the floor dropped quickly away from him. He struggled briefly, but then recognized the scent of the boy.

There was the odd smell of cloth — of a shirt — but there was also the sweet, slightly soapy smell of the boy's skin, the distinctive oil of his hair, the warm damp of his breath, and a sharp smell coming from something shiny on his wrist. Sheldon squirmed so that he could dig his small soft claws into the boy's shirt and gripped the boy's finger excitedly in his tiny teeth. The boy giggled, lifted Sheldon up so that his head was against the boy's neck just below his jaw. The boy made a lot of complicated noises, but at that moment Sheldon felt completely safe and happy.

There was then a never-ending companionship: Sheldon and the boy. They chased marbles around the floor. Sheldon chased the end of a belt dragged down the hallway by the boy. The boy put down Sheldon's food, then sat and watched while he ate it. The boy would lie on the grass outside, while Sheldon, ears cocked forward, listened for prey that was unwisely trying to hide under dandelions, in tufty patches the mower missed, under leaves fallen from the big maple. In the evening, the boy was allowed to watch some television, and Sheldon would stretch out next to the boy's thigh and have his ears rubbed. When it was bedtime, the boy would always leave his door open a crack, and Sheldon could get one paw through, then squeeze into the room, haul himself up onto the bed, and sleep next to the boy's feet or on his hair or in the crevice between the pillows.

Summer turned to autumn, and there were ample leaves to chase and piles of them to dive into. Autumn turned to winter, and Sheldon loved jumping into deep fluffy snow, shaking it off his nose when his head emerged, causing the boy to make such happy noises. Winter turned to spring, and then there were bugs. It was the flies that raised the killer instinct in Sheldon, buzzing and bumbling everywhere. Sheldon chased them through the house with determination, cornered them against window panes, then crushed and ate them. Spring turned to summer again, and then the whole series of patterns came round once more.

It was not always good. Sometimes playing became just too exciting and the boy would be hurt. Sheldon would then sneak away, sit in a corner somewhere, and worry about what had gone wrong. The boy's mother was not always pleased to have Sheldon around. When she was busy, she got into a bad mood easily, and she would often kick Sheldon out of her way. The first time this happened, Sheldon panicked, scrabbled to run — couldn't get out of the kitchen fast enough — ran to the boy's room and hid under his bed right back against the wall.

Then one day, everything changed. The boy was no longer around during the day. Sheldon played by himself, but it wasn't the same. There was always sleep, and he could sleep almost the whole day without even trying. So Sheldon had to be satisfied with just a bit of the boy's time, in the evenings. It was okay, but it wasn't the same.

Sheldon was getting older, and his food changed. The food before had been strong tasting, delicious. The new food was not. But Sheldon got used to it. He found that he was sick less often, but then he didn't go outside nearly as much with the boy, where he used to find his way among the tall grass at the bottom of the garden, eat a few shoots of the broad green blades, and within a few minutes disgorge a large lump of fur. He always felt much better after that, and on the whole he enjoyed eating grass, but somehow there was no need now that he had his new food.

What he had more trouble with was the pain in his mouth. It came and went, but as time went by, Sheldon found that it was harder to eat the dry kibble that was always in his third bowl. His first bowl was for soft food, his second for water, and his third for kibble. They always had to be in the same places, and while the boy understood this, his mother didn't seem to, and Sheldon was sometimes given unfriendly pokes from the toe of her shoe when he waited for the bowls to be moved to the right spots.

One of the things Sheldon liked particularly was going in the car. The best was going to the family's country place. Sheldon had ridden in the car for as long as he could remember, and he didn't need to be asked twice to climb in, where he took his regular seat on the back window ledge. He found it very exciting at first. Things went by fast, far faster than they did when he was running in the garden, and he worked hard trying to see what it was that was whooshing by so quickly. It didn't take long for him to realize that they were moving too fast, and his routine became a matter of taking his place on the back window ledge, spending a few minutes getting used to the flying images, then curling up and going to sleep.

It seemed that the boy had less and less time for Sheldon. After dinner, he often sat in his room doing something with a pencil, and when Sheldon tried to play with the pencil or tried to climb onto the boy's lap, he was pushed away. So he contented himself with finding a place to sleep in the sun on a window ledge or in a corner of the sofa or on the boy's bed when the boy was away during the day.

For some time, Sheldon had noticed that he could no longer jump easily. He walked with a slight limp, and in the morning, if he jumped down off a bed or the sofa too soon after he awoke, there was a good deal of pain in one of his legs. This made Sheldon less even-tempered, because one of his favourite activities, chasing flies, now brought him pain rather than pleasure and the thrill of victory. When the pain came to him at night, as it did occasionally, he would complain, and an impatient and unfriendly voice would be raised somewhere in the house. There was one time when the boy made to pick him up but somehow caused his leg to turn suddenly. Sheldon screamed and hissed at the boy; he was immediately sorry, but it was too late. The boy put him down onto the bed and walked away. He also lashed out at the boy's mother one day when she prodded him strongly with the toe of her shoe. The pain flared up and he grabbed at her ankle, claws bared. The shouting this produced was frightening, and Sheldon just managed to make it under the bed to the far corner and well away from that vindictive toe of her shoe.

One pleasant day in autumn when everyone was at home, Sheldon's pain had eased and he hoped that maybe it had gone for good. Sheldon was sleeping in the sun when he was picked up and carried out to the car. This was an unexpected pleasure. He hadn't been in the car for some time, and he quickly took his place on the back window ledge. There was the usual brief effort to catch sight of things passing, then Sheldon curled up and went to sleep. Soon, the car doors opened and everyone got out. Sheldon jumped down off the back window onto the seat, onto the floor, and then out onto the ground. Immediately he was among tall grasses. This was exciting and hadn't happened for a while. Sheldon stalked his way through some very tall rustly weeds, listened for things crawling under leaves, had a very satisfying pee, even ate some grass. Sheldon knew this wasn't where they usually stopped, so he turned to go back to the car. Funny. No car. Sheldon retraced his steps, found his own scent on the ground, turned and tried again, but still no car. He decided to wait, and while he waited, he would do some more exploring.

Sheldon explored a great deal and it was all very intriguing. There were smells he recalled only vaguely. But when Sheldon looked at the shadows, he began to have deep uneasy feelings, almost as though those patches of darkness were old dreams that he might or might not have had. He was concerned about things in the sky and about large animals on the ground, which he might not hear coming.

Sheldon climbed a tree.

He was not worried. He would wait for the boy. The boy would come back. The boy always came back.

Norwegian Wood

There was a lot to do.

He had a curling match at ten, then lunch with friends at one, and at five thirty he would be getting together with Rob and Marshall for drinks, steaks, and baked potatoes cooked on Rob's grill. He looked at the note on his fridge door, in Rob's hand. 'Steve, bring pie, whipped cream, red wine.' Wine bought, pie made yesterday, cream to be whipped this afternoon. Then, no doubt, the evening would enjoy its usual slide into tipsy hilarity as they watched a couple of Pink Panther movies. But despite all that, there was no rush. He had always been an early riser, and today not only was no exception — it was an exemplary beginning.

It wasn't so much dawn as it was a deluge of light — flowing over the top of the low-rise building opposite and tumbling into his kitchen and living room in an uncontrolled torrent. It was warm on his bare chest, arms, and face and demonstrated yet again that shoulders did not provide an exclusive connection between sunlight and happiness.

While he was pondering what would constitute breakfast, he collected the morning paper and carefully looked through it for the one or two pieces of good or quirky news that were always there, someplace. Eggs? Maybe not. Toast? Definitely. Apple butter on the toast? Things were definitely looking up. Bacon? Do bears shit in the—

He moved across the room and picked up the phone.

"Marshall! ... Yes, I'm up and alive and looking forward to tonight. ... What? ... Of course, I'm bringing pie! ... What? ... No, you old bugger, I'm not going deaf, you're mumbling into the phone from the next room! ... Yes. That's better. ... Well, you don't need to have any pie. ... No, my pies are not too big, they're standard-sized pies. ... Let me give you some advice. Take that tape measure and burn it. ... Well, my advice is, *fuck your doctor*. ... Yes, sorry. I forgot that she's twenty-eight. ... I don't doubt for a minute that you could handle a twenty-eight-year-old. ... Until half past five. Thanks for calling, Marshall."

The bacon was the good stuff — firm and smoky and having an honest rind, not that flaccid pink putty from the supermarket, pumped full of water. He had once measured a pound of supermarket bacon before and after cooking, and had taken care to condense the water so he could measure the amounts of water and fat released, at which point they weighed together twice as much as the pathetic strips of edible material. Today would see the last of the bacon used, so he added that to his list. There would be time to go shopping after lunch, and the list had now crept up to eight or nine items. The situation was calling out for a trip to the market, something else to look forward to, especially when one added in the usual kibitzing with Mel at the meat counter, Maria at Atlantic Fish, and Jonesey at the cheese shop. He found that there was no way he could get out of the market in less than an hour and still observe all the social graces. He often spent two hours there, since Mel alone could wax lyrical for half an hour on a single kind of sausage.

But, enough of this. The bacon was in the pan, the bread was in the toaster (the whisky was in the jar, hee! hee!), the aroma of coffee was filling the kitchen, his juice and vitamin pills were laid out, and a long item in today's paper was calling out to him — a piece about the return of the gingko tree from obscurity — offering a half hour of communion.

He took advantage of the few moments to lay out his curling gear, including the cap everyone considered so dashing. He also laid out his notebook and malachite pen. When he made notes during the matches, it always agitated Leslie, with whom he had psychological scores to settle, and his malachite variation on the Chinese water torture was just the ticket.

The morning's vitamin pills slid down on a rivulet of guava juice, one of his favourites, he poured a cup of coffee and added milk, then settled down to the gingko story. Tales of renascence always left him with a warm feeling.

The sound of the toaster induced him to get the butter from the fridge and a knife. The wooden toast tongs were where they always lived, in the front compartment of the top drawer immediately to the right of the sink. He retrieved them and lifted the toast from the toaster onto the plate.

At first, he couldn't believe it.

Shock. Then a feeling of ... disconnection? Loss?

The toast tongs were in three pieces in his hand. They had just ... fallen asunder. And it looked as though no number of king's horses and men...

When had it been? 1972. They were just nineteen. They had somehow scraped together enough money for what then seemed like super-cheap airfares to London. They had got themselves to Somerset, lived on next to nothing in lodgings that were primitive but clean and then went to the Glastonbury Festival. It had been fantastic, liberating, and for the two of them, unifying. They never forgot it. And that's where the tongs had come from.

They wanted a memento. Just something to remind them they had been there. There was no expectation at the time of this being anything other than a transient reminder, no hope of something permanent or having lasting meaning.

They were just toast tongs. A quirky notional impulse. The guy they bought them from said the tongs had been made by an artisan woodworker who lived near Bergen, and they were ready to believe it, even though it was almost certainly bullshit. In the end, it didn't matter who had made them or where they were made. The tongs lasted and took up residence in their home and in their lives. From the beginning, or so it had seemed, they became infused with meaning. The toast tongs were soon recognized as a Glastonbury mascot, a symbol of an event, a spirit of the time, as meaningful as the engagement rings they had given each other on the plane during the flight to London. The tongs had darkened from age, but they had been with them for — how long now? — more than forty-five years.

Then there was that visit to the doctor, and a short eight months later, she was gone, taken from him.

He looked at his breakfast spread out on the table.

It would be good, and he was looking forward to it, still. Curling would be as companionable and as much fun as ever. Lunch would be very enjoyable. It always was. And the evening would be one long belly laugh, plus the usual amount of personal roasting and off-colour repartee. It was all good, and he would enjoy it.

But there was no use pretending.

Nothing would ever be the same again.

Not without Norma.

Pools

His earliest recollections were of flowers.

There was his own bed of marigolds, even though his mother did all the work. And he recalled as well how the little ants worked so assiduously on the fat peony buds before they opened in all their flamboyant red and white garments. And the sweet peas that climbed their trellis to pose coquettishly. And the delicate white flowers on the potato plants — how he worked, long and indignantly, picking off those grotesque and arrogant potato bugs. And the elegant yellow tomato flowers — he was repulsed by the fat, hideous tomato worms. But most of all the daffodils — how they cast their glances down demurely, whispered, swayed and smiled together, as though one of them had just discovered a four-leafed clover. Especially the daffodils.

He also remembered lying in the grass when he was very young, in his shorts and T-shirt, the ants and bugs climbing his bare legs and arms, and as he gazed up through leaves and branches, he marvelled at all the battleships, tugboats, tumbling boulders, misshapen toads, hippopotami, bearded heads of old men, wrecked cars — all of them masquerading as clouds.

His mother had chosen the land their house was built upon, although his father really would have liked something different. His father would have liked flamboyant flower beds, a tennis court, severely trimmed hedges, and a croquet lawn. The piece of land they eventually agreed on was far more dramatic.

It was a largish plot having deep rich soil. On the north and east was a loosely planted natural cedar wood with wide avenues damped to anechoic standard by an underpadding made from decades of cedar leaves. To the south, the soil yielded first to a flat expanse of bare limestone, but then everything tumbled down a thirty-foot embankment ornamented by large and ancient water-carved crags to a narrow path along the river's edge. This embankment became his mother's very large rock garden, and her years of love's labour, definitely not lost, had coaxed from it an artist's palette of floral brilliance threaded by switchback paths alongside which sat small benches built into the rock and well-chosen for their views.

Three natural springs bubbled from this rocky embankment, and his mother had created channels to guide their flows to a common point about ten feet above the level of the river, where she had a stonemason construct a pool on a small natural plateau. After two or three years, moss, grasses, and little delicate flowers had encroached onto the stone defining the borders of this pool, slowly erasing signs of a human hand and eventually reclaiming it as Nature's own creation.

Next to this pool was a bench cut out of the rock and covered by a thick veneer of limestone slabs, oriented so that someone seated there looked down and out over the river. The rough edges of the stone had been ground smooth, and here Nature also began reclamation right away, adding darkness and patina in a matter of months. When he came here, as he did regularly, armed with cushions, this bench made a superb reading couch, and often he could be found there with a copy of *Kidnapped* or one of the Hardy Boys books or *The Little Prince* or *Journey to the Centre of the Earth* or *King Solomon's Mines* or any of the dozens of other books written by men who were really boys at heart. To lie here in solitude, to read, to be bathed in sunlight and kissed by puffs of air rising flirtatiously from the river, to hear the spring water scheming in whispers as it tumbled down to the pool, to see the coloured stones in the bottom of the pool shimmer and dance through the ripples, occasionally to lean down over the pool and take a cool, fresh draught, it was all about as close to Arcadia as one was likely to get.

Only much later did he learn that his mother had taken dozens, perhaps a couple of hundred, photos of him near this pool. *My little Byron*, as she described him, and his clear skin, deep expressive eyes, and unruly flaxen hair lent him that universal appeal of the golden youth, reminiscent indeed of Bryon or Keats or Brooke.

Although he was a quiet lad, his mother had made certain he had a good social presence, and it was clear that most of the other mothers secretly doted on him and would have had him as their own. Not only during his early childhood but all through school, into his adolescence and even into early adulthood, he radiated that same serene, complete, self-contained detachment, and his quiet manners, slow smile, and aura of dreamy but acute awareness set him aside from others, even as those others were more than willing to include him in their circles. He was a natural student and he did very well.

At the age of twenty-eight, he was left on his own by the deaths, within a few months of each other, of his father and mother. This was a serious shock, and he struggled for several years to come to terms with these events, to find a new equilibrium.

In the end, he emerged a somewhat changed person. He had finished his studies by then, but having inherited everything from his parents, he had options. The option he chose, with very little apparent reflection, was a life similar to the one he had led to that point, and it was only much later that he realized what he had done with his time.

He lived into old age, and his death in a quiet hospice was as serene as his life had been. It was then that the revelations had begun.

He had left behind, neatly and carefully organized and placed in storage, a set of notes and documents that filled thirty-three filing boxes. Nineteen of these were filled by poems and fragments of poems, along with a request to publish those worthy of being published. They were exquisite, strong but delicate, forceful but delightful, masterful but reclusive, forward but pensive, modern but timeless. They were written in all the ageless but bygone poetic forms.

In the remaining boxes were thousands of photos from many countries, organized carefully by time and place, a visual account of his lifelong devotion to pools, fountains, streams, and springs. They included vigorous mountain streams, quiet shaded country pools, and fountains — large and small, dramatic and demure, in open spaces and secluded courtyards, in small and large gardens.

In one of these boxes were the photographs his mother had taken, lovingly framed and labelled, and stored with care away from the light. In these photos, the Arcadian rock garden of his boyhood lived on. In the last folder within this box, there were pictures of flowers.

Quiet, seductive, delicate, standing in groups with mosses and grasses lying in anticipation at their feet — the flowers, leaning over slightly, gazed into a crystal-clear pool.

Fuller

Fuller.

Clark hated his name. Not his first name. Not even his middle name. It was his last name that caused him such trouble.

Fuller.

All through school, he was the guy who hawked brushes. In the school cafeteria, the same people who tortured him about how many brushes he had sold that day, asked him at the end of lunch whether he was "fuller" now.

Then there was the day when his arch enemy, the guy who always wore a smirk, Nigel Bloody Atherton, never let up — went on and on and on, until finally, during the middle of a baseball game at recess, Clark dropped his bat, walked calmly to the pitcher's mound where Atherton stood sneering, gave him a tremendous punch in the mouth, then kicked him three times after he had fallen.

Of course there were consequences. The most significant and the most satisfying was that Atherton had lost two teeth. Atherton was given a detention, but Clark was given a week of detentions and a letter home threatening expulsion if there were any repeat of that incident. It was unfair but almost worth it. In some ways, the worst by far was the pep talk from Mr. Baxter. He addressed the entire class.

"This has to stop. The sort of bullying that caused this incident ends here. Do you all underst—"

"But I didn't bully him!" Atherton exclaimed in the aggrieved tone of a privileged brat.

"Interrupt me again, Atherton, and you will also receive a week of detentions! As I was saying, there is no place in this school for bullying, ridiculing, gang-teasing, mocking — they're all different faces of the same thing. From today, if I catch anyone — *anyone* — engaging in this ridiculous nonsense, that person will have a note sent home to their parents. Do you all understand me quite clearly?"

Mr. Baxter looked severely around the room.

"As for the events of this week, I'm ashamed of you all. Any of you could have acted to stop this. Particularly, I'm ashamed of Atherton and Fuller, but more Atherton. What Fuller did was inexcusable, but he was driven to it by Atherton."

Atherton tensed in his seat and his mouth began to open.

"Careful, Atherton!" Mr. Baxter warned. "You are *this close!*"

"I hardly think I need remind you, Fuller, and indeed remind all of you, that physical violence is completely intolerable. You are all expected to behave, and you *will* behave, as polite young people. You are not uncivilized wild animals and you will not behave as such. Am I making myself entirely clear?"

His gaze scanned the room, like a death ray that was loaded, cocked, and ready to fire.

"Now. The specific instance here is your mocking of Fuller. Don't think that I'm unaware of what's going on. I will go as far as to say that I have some slight — very slight mind you — sympathy for Fuller. After all, he can't help that his name is Fuller."

Clark didn't hear any of the rest of Mr. Baxter's harangue. That statement cut like red-hot steel. Even the teacher, *even the teacher*, felt that Fuller was an odd, silly, comical name!

Three weeks later, Mr. Baxter quietly asked Clark to stay behind in the classroom for a few minutes at recess. "What's wrong, Clark?"

"Nothing, sir."

"Well, I think it's more than nothing. You're one of the best students in the class, but for the past while you've said nothing, volunteered no answers, asked no questions. Something has changed."

Clark fidgeted, looked at his shoes, and Mr. Baxter let the silence lengthen. Eventually, Clark raised his eyes and looked directly at his teacher.

"The teasing has stopped, sir, but only because they're all afraid of you. Apart from that, nothing has changed. Atherton still smirks at me. And I can see in the others' eyes that they really would like to ask me, the guy they regarded as 'the Fuller Brush Man', how many brushes I've sold."

Clark paused here, wondering if he should say what he was thinking, but then he decided that he had to. "Even you, sir, you see me as a Fuller Brush Man."

Clark expected a serious, angry response to this, so he was surprised when nothing happened. He was even more surprised when Mr. Baxter sat back, and a mellow look came over his face. He looked at Clark for some time, then said something that, in retrospect, changed Clark's life.

"Do you know what a *baxter* is, Clark?"

Clark didn't know what to say. He sat there, looking blankly at his teacher, who looked back at Clark pleasantly.

After a long delay, Mr. Baxter said, "A baxter is a baker or perhaps a brewer. Do you know what a *fuller* is? And do you know what fullers, weavers, websters, tuckers, and walkers have in common?"

After not quite such a long delay, Clark said, "No, I don't."

"They're all associated with an old profession — making cloth. Have you heard of fuller's earth?"

"No, sir."

Mr. Baxter sat looking at Clark pleasantly for a while longer, then rose and began walking around slowly.

"People have forgotten one of the primary reasons, possibly the most important reason, why we have schools and why young people are forced to attend them until they are at least sixteen years old. That reason is to banish ignorance. This whole business of bullying and teasing is a tragic instance of ignorance joining forces with bad manners and leading to the most astonishing levels of stupidity."

Mr. Baxter's expression softened from the schoolmaster to someone who was settling in for a nice chat with Clark.

"You are most likely not aware of this, Clark, but you have been particularly favoured. Every one of your names — Clark, Bowman, and Fuller — identifies a profession or a social standing."

They talked for another few minutes, until the end of recess. They talked again at the end of the day, for another half hour. And again several times more that week.

Mr. Baxter began passing copies of articles to Clark. He received four altogether, over a period of about four weeks. Clark read each one carefully after it had been passed to him, then he read all four several times. He had three long discussions with Mr. Baxter about these articles, and Mr. Baxter also passed to Clark the names of several books he could look for when he was near a good public library.

The immediate effect of this reading and study was to give Clark an entirely fresh outlook. He realized that his names traced back through history following three distinct occupations, one of which was skilled, another epic, and all of them distinctive and interesting. Bearing the middle name Bowman meant that in some sense he traced back to the glory days of Crécy and Agincourt. The thought that he should be upset by all the rude jibes from ignorant classmates now seemed completely absurd. This was reflected, he was told later, in his newfound confidence among the other students. When any of them smirked or looked at him oddly, he just smiled at them, and he could see the puzzlement and confusion on their faces. On more than one occasion, he wiped the smirk off Atherton's face by comments that Atherton was ignorant and to be pitied or that even having to deal with him was just a tedious waste of time or something similar. On many occasions he made as though Atherton simply was not there.

In not many more years, they were out of school. Clark lost touch with all but the two or three who went on to university. Clark excelled, devoured university life, and never looked back. By the age of twenty-seven, he had spent time in two post-doctoral positions. By thirty-five, he had worked his way into the lower management levels of a largish publishing operation. By forty, he was a literary agent and an author in his own right.

Now, having built a solid business, he reflected on all this as he looked at the two books standing at one side of his desk. His name, as author, Clark B. Fuller, beamed back at him from their spines. It seemed incredible. Twenty-five years. He had lost touch with Mr. Baxter long ago, but he still had a manila folder where he kept the four now very yellowed copies of articles that Mr. Baxter had given him.

In his professional life, Clark always received a good deal of mail, but the envelope that arrived one day bearing the logo and name for Otonabee District High School was unexpected. Out of curiosity, he opened it first. It was an invitation to speak at the annual meeting of school alumni and students. Clark was intrigued. A quick telephone conversation with the principal provided some background, and how and why his name had been chosen. Clark said he would get back to the principal shortly and provide an answer, but he already knew that he would accept.

Clark did a bit of research and found that about ten of his former classmates were still around, the rest having moved away, died, or were of unknown whereabouts. Three of his former teachers still lived locally, and he was surprised and pleased to see that one of them was Jonathan Baxter. There were a few points of detail to settle about the alumni meeting, and he raised his few questions in a short email to the principal, adding at the bottom, *Do you know whether Mr. Baxter will be present?*

The day of the alumni meeting rolled around. Clark would make his presentation in the late afternoon, there would then be dinner, followed by a period of socializing that would begin at eight o'clock and go on as long as people remained interested. A few days before the event, Clark received a list of attendees. A small number of current students, about fifteen, would attend. Clark found the number of alumni to be surprisingly large, and they were about evenly distributed between those who were older and those who were younger than Clark. Four of his contemporaries were on the list, and one of these was Atherton. In his motel room, as he dressed for the evening, Clark found that he was moderately excited.

His talk went well. Clark was a good speaker, and his witticisms, his humorous stories from the past, and his more serious observations about his time at the school were well received. Toward the end of his talk, he spoke about teachers and the role they play, concluding that "teachers have the difficult task of trying to prepare students for life, when the future challenges are things that nobody can foresee. But an equally important role of teachers is to make students aware of the vast, shimmering, intoxicating body of knowledge that the human race has amassed and to awaken in those students a realization of the great potential for intellectual excitement, personal satisfaction, and professional fulfillment that this knowledge represents. A teacher who can do this is a good teacher, and a good teacher can change your life. I had such a teacher. He is here tonight, and I want to say how very grateful I am to Jonathan Baxter."

Everyone looked to one side of the room where a white-haired man, somewhat frail but erect and alert, sat and made no effort to dry or conceal the tears that were flowing down his cheeks.

Applause began slowly, but then was strong and sustained.

Afterwards, Clark and Mr. Baxter stood shaking hands.

"I hope I didn't embarrass you, Jonathan", Clark said.

"No, not at all. I was overwhelmed and you were very generous, but I wasn't embarrassed."

They stood talking for some time. Before they moved on to speak to other attendees, they arranged a follow-up dinner some weeks in the future.

Clark moved through the friendly crowd, and many thanked him for a very nice speech. At one point, he turned to find himself next to Atherton and Mr. Baxter.

"Hello Nigel", Clark said pleasantly.

"Hello, er, Dr. Fuller."

"Clark is good enough", Clark said smiling.

"I'm a bit surprised that you — remember me, er, Clark."

"I remember most of the kids who were students with me. Hard to think why I shouldn't. It is strange, though, to see the old school again", and here Clark looked around slowly.

There was a slightly strained pause at that point. "Is this your first time back — first time back to the school?" Atherton asked.

"Yes, I'm a bit ashamed to say that it is."

A tray of dessert nibbles drifted by, and Clark turned to take one.

"Do you ever think about those days when we were students here?" Atherton asked.

"Yes. Sometimes."

"You probably hate me", Atherton said, this time a bit too quickly.

"No, Nigel! Why would I hate you?"

"Well, I-I was pretty horrible."

Clark laughed. "That was all a long time ago. There's been a lot of water flow under the bridge since then. No, I tend to remember the good things."

They talked a bit longer, and Atherton persevered, despite the fact that he was not completely at ease. In due course, Mr. Baxter joined in and they discussed local matters. Clark had nothing to say because local matters were an unknown to him, but Atherton relaxed visibly. As he was listening, Clark suddenly realized something.

Atherton's world was very small. Smaller than Clark would have imagined. Clark looked at Atherton and Mr. Baxter, and he knew suddenly, vividly — and depressingly — that what he had said in his remarks about the great store of human knowledge was true to a degree that he had almost not appreciated. Atherton had missed out on almost all that, and from Clark's point of view, it would be little better than imprisonment to live in a world as limited as Atherton's.

Clark smiled inwardly at how surprises can leap at one from the past, at how something apparently long known can show a new and unanticipated face, at the power and subtlety of irony.

The three of them were bound together and yet held unalterably apart by the implications flowing from three different perceived realities tied to just a single word:

Fuller.

This story was inspired by my own primary school teachers, three of whom stand out as gifted and perceptive: Mr. McGibbon, Mr. Fullerton, and Mr. Brown.

New Faces

Harry had met Jack in a fairly unlikely way: they had both been witnesses to an inept attempt at robbing a bank.

The bank's security system had thwarted the would-be robber, who claimed to have a handgun but didn't. As witnesses, Harry and Jack were asked to stay around until the police arrived and they struck up a conversation while they waited. Harry asked Jack if he would like to meet sometime for a drink; the excitement of the moment had got Jack much more charged than usual, and he agreed right away, and just for good measure, they exchanged telephone numbers. They chose a time and place, and talked about what each other did until the police said they weren't needed any further because there was evidence on tape, plenty of bank employees as witnesses, and a good chance that the miscreant would cave under questioning anyway — which, they found out not too much later, he did.

The date of their meeting was only four days after the bank excitement, but long before that, in fact before Jack had even got home, he was having misgivings about meeting Harry again and going to a bar he hadn't heard of before. Misgivings in general about disruptions to his established and comfortable routines. But it would have been far more stressful to call Harry and try to present a credible excuse for why he couldn't make it. So he went.

The Factory sounded not at all like Jack's cup of tea, and from the outside, it looked even less so. Along the street outside were parked high end BMWs, Audis, Mercedes, and a Porsche. Jack felt himself to be at a watershed, or maybe beershed or decisionshed would have been more appropriate. A timorous interior voice advised him to turn around and go home, but he knew he really shouldn't, couldn't stand up Harry so blatantly. So, full of trepidation and laden by the imagined weight of numerous anticipatory I-told-you-so concerns, he opened the door and entered. His gaze was met by warm brickwork, large ceiling beams, reasonable lighting (requiring neither night-vision goggles nor sunglasses), and a surprisingly civilized noise level.

Harry stood up from the bar and beamed a huge smile and big wave at Jack. They greeted each other and Harry asked what Jack would like to drink, nodded approval at his choice of Mill Street Tankhouse Ale, ordered two, and they found a small table in a corner away from the major traffic flows.

"Good to see you again, Jack. Did you have any trouble finding the place?"

"Oh. No."

"It didn't take you long to get here, I hope."

"Oh. No. I live close."

"So do I. Almost just around the corner, in fact. Where is your place?"

"Oh. Just on Adelaide. Near Jarvis."

"In that row of heritage buildings? On the north side? Or in the new building to the east of Jarvis?"

"In the heritage buildings."

"Fantastic! Well, cheers!"

"Cheers", Jack said modestly and took a sip.

Harry mentioned the flashy cars outside. Jack said that they were odd vehicles for pub patrons. Harry laughed. "They aren't here for the pub. The offices of a publisher are on the third floor."

Jack looked puzzled. "I didn't realize that authors did so well these days."

Harry roared again. "Those cars belong to agents and publicists, not authors. The authors are almost beggars."

Jack wondered how Harry knew all this.

They sat in silence for a while, and after a moment, Jack began wondering and worrying whether this would be one of those occasions when nobody could think of anything to say and a long period of social discomfort has to crawl by slowly until one of you looks at his watch and utters some escape line, like "I guess my laundry will be done by now" or "I need to buy some new socks" or "I just remembered I left the fridge door open."

Harry took another manly swig of his beer and smiled at Jack.

"That was something different at the bank the other day, wasn't it?" Jack said, almost conspiratorially, flashing the smile of a remembered adventure that only the two of them shared. "I told my colleagues at work, but it took me a good fifteen minutes to convince them I wasn't just blowing smoke. They believed me in the end when I showed them this…" And here Harry showed Jack a picture on his cell phone. In the background was the hopeful bank robber being taken into custody by a burly policeman. In the foreground, to Jack's complete astonishment, was — Jack! "I probably wasn't supposed to take this, but I wanted a record of the day."

They both took another drink of beer.

"I don't suppose you've ever been at the scene of a bank robbery before, have you Jack?"

"Oh. No."

Harry smiled at Jack and asked how long he had lived in the area.

"Long time?"

"Sorry?" Jack said.

"How long have you lived there?"

Jack's expression cleared. "Oh. Ten years."

They each took another sip of beer.

"What do you do, Jack? Or are you retired?"

"Oh. Yes. Retired."

"And when you worked. What did you do?"

"Oh. Family lawyer."

By this time, Jack was feeling much more at ease, because although Harry's questions were not at all the kind of conversational fare Jack was used to, he found that Harry had a very sympathetic style. But then a thought occurred to Jack: *I don't really have any conversational fare. I don't converse with anybody from one week to the next.* He looked around the pub. It was moderately busy, but quiet. There were small groups of people talking. Jack felt somewhat self-conscious, couldn't remember the last time he had been in a pub. But, looking around he realized that nobody was paying attention to him. He wasn't out of place. Harry was relaxed and friendly and didn't become anxious when a conversational lull settled over them.

"What do you do, Harry?"

Jack was completely surprised at hearing his own voice, to the extent that he almost looked around to see if somebody else had asked the question.

"I'm an investment analyst", Harry said and then went on to talk about where he worked, how long he had worked there, and what he hoped to be doing a couple of years from now.

By this time, Harry had finished his beer, and Jack, to his own surprise, had finished three-quarters of his.

"Same again, Harry?" Jack asked.

"Yes. But I can get it."

"Oh. No. That's fine", Jack said, and picking up Harry's glass, he moved off to the bar.

Jack carried the two filled glasses back to their table, they settled themselves, and intoned "Cheers!"

Jack surprised himself once again by asking if Harry was married.

"Divorced. You?"

"Was. Janice died many years ago. Cancer."

A wave of genuine sympathy swept across Harry's face. "I'm sorry."

Jack indicated by a wave of his hand that it was all ancient history, they each took another sip of beer and waited for that cloud to blow over.

"What do you do now?" Harry asked, in a way that made Jack feel, to his own surprise, that he wanted to answer rather than clam up. But he didn't really know where to start.

"Oh. Not much."

Harry's expression beamed an appealing mixture of interest, empathy, and curiosity, and Jack began to elaborate, almost before he had decided to do so.

"I read a lot. Three friends and I have a small book club. I do a lot of walking. I attend quite a few free lectures." Jack scooped a small handful of peanuts from the bowl in front of him and munched while looking around the room. "Sounds pretty boring, even to me, when I say it like that. But I'm not bored."

"I doubt you're bored", Harry said mildly. "People become restive over short periods, but that's pretty normal. If a person is bored continuously over a long period, that's not good. In fact, it's dangerous. I suspect that people are just very adaptable, and they adjust to whatever their situation is."

Harry hesitated here, and Jack cast him what he hoped was an encouraging glance.

"I don't have time to get bored, Jack, but when I hear people say things like you've just said, about having time for reading and walking and stuff like that, I do become a tad jealous."

They both drank again.

Harry set down his glass. "This might be the wrong timing, but I'm wondering whether you'd be interested in sitting in on a small informal group we've set up. We meet about once every two or three weeks for drinks and nibbles. It's just shooting the breeze, but they're an interesting bunch."

"Oh. I don't know", Jack said after a long hesitation. "I doubt I would fit in. I'm probably thirty years older than the oldest of you. Perhaps more."

"No, I think they would all like the variety. You could try it once, and if you didn't like it, nobody would be offended." Harry saw that Jack was see-sawing. "Go ahead!" Harry said, encouraging Jack by tone of voice and gesture to be a devil.

"Oh. I don't know."

His brow slightly furrowed, Jack looked steadily at Harry. Jack felt the same internal confusion that appeared on his face, a blend of social nervousness and mild interest.

"When do you meet? And where?" Jack asked hesitantly.

"That's the stuff!" Harry said. "As it happens, we meet here, and we usually sit over there." Harry pointed toward a largish alcove on one side of the room. "And we always meet on a Wednesday evening."

Jack hesitated even longer, and Harry just sat there looking encouraging.

"How many are there?"

"Never more than eight. Usually four or five. We're meeting next Wednesday. Why not give it a whirl?"

"Oh. Can I think about it and give you a call?"

"Certainly!" Harry pulled a business card out of his shirt pocket. "Probably best to call me at my home number after eight in the evening. During the day, things are typically very hectic. But you don't really need to call ahead. Just turn up."

"Thanks", Jack said and slipped the card into his pocket.

They finished their pints, talked a bit more, sat a bit more in companionable silence, and then paid and left. Outside the pub, they shook hands.

"It was a real pleasure to get to know you a little better, Jack. Remember, next Wednesday. We meet here at eight, usually leave by ten. If I don't hear from you, I'll look for you here."

As Jack half-expected, he spent hours during the intervening days wondering whether to go to the pub meeting or not, and swinging back and forth along the decision line, from mild enthusiasm in favour to sweaty apprehension against. At one extreme, he was just about decided. "They won't bite," he told himself, "and it wouldn't hurt you to get out more, break the current stale pattern." At the other extreme, he was equally decided. "You're just being a silly old fool", he admonished himself. "These are young men. You'll have nothing in common with them, and that will make you all uncomfortable. Give Harry a call now and say thanks but no thanks."

But he continued to dither until it was too late. At twenty to eight on the appointed evening, he pocketed the one implement he would need and then set out for The Factory. He arrived at ten to eight. The place was less than half full, but there was a happy buzz of discussion.

Jack looked at the alcove. Empty. Not even Harry was here.

All right, said the negative ogre inside him. *Turn around now and get out of here while you can.*

But still Jack hesitated, scanned the room once again to check that Harry wasn't somewhere else, that he'd missed him. No Harry. He thought about just going and sitting in the alcove and waiting. But then what if Harry wasn't the first to turn up? What if Harry hadn't told the others that Jack was coming? Even worse, what if Harry was ill and didn't turn up at all?

This was all becoming too complicated, and Jack was beginning to lean toward a quick exit.

"Jack! Hey, Jack! I'm glad you could make it!"

Harry came over, all friendly smiles, his right hand extended.

"Sorry I wasn't here when you arrived. Needed a quick trip to the whizzer. Let's sit down and order. Have you eaten?"

"Oh. Yes."

"Just wanted to check. We don't usually eat here, but I didn't want you starting off out of step."

They sat in the alcove. The enclosed space muted some of the background buzz in the larger room, while the slight echo from the alcove walls made the space feel oddly familiar, cosy. The dark wood and the lighting — not too bright and not too dim, as before — made the alcove a welcoming place.

An oddity, although Harry had warned him of this during their previous discussion, was that the group did observe one rule.

Drinks came in threes only. If you drank beer, you had to have three glasses. Not two. Not four. Three. Same for whisky. Three glasses. If you wanted more, you had to order three more or switch to something else, but then you had to have three glasses of that.

Jack was not at all sure about his ability to down three pints of beer. Or rather, he was quite confident that he would not be able to. But he had come prepared.

Three other youngish men arrived over the next fifteen minutes. Jack guessed that they were all in their early to mid-thirties. Introductions were made, and conversations sprang up spontaneously.

A tray of beer glasses arrived and they were distributed around the table. Just as one of the men reached for his pint, Jack took a largish whisky glass from his jacket pocket and poured a third of his beer into it. The others looked on in puzzlement.

"Oh. I'm here as a guest", Jack said diffidently. "Three pints is likely beyond me. But I can manage three, or even six, of these glasses quite well."

"Bravo!" one of the men said past a beaming smile. "Harry! Where have you been hiding this chap all these years? He's a natural! That's what I call observing the rule not only in spirit but with class!"

From then, Jack was pleased to feel no sense of discomfort at being a new guy in the alcove. They all took their turns asking Jack a question here, a question there, and Jack replied in his usual economy — the only word he used liberally being "oh." There were long spells when Jack just sat back and listened, and that seemed to be fine with everyone. By ten o'clock, he had a clutch of business cards, knew a little about each of them, was pleasantly surprised to find that among them they had quite a wide range of interests, and was even more pleased to have encountered almost no shop talk, which he knew he would have found incomprehensible. Outside, they all shook hands amid smiles and laughter, and strode off into the night.

On the short walk back to his place, Jack thought, *Well, that was all right.* But, in fact, he knew that it was different from being just "all right" — he had been given something to think about.

A week later, Harry was mildly surprised to receive an email from Jack. Jack had seemed to him the kind of guy who probably didn't even own a computer.

Nice to hear from you Jack. I didn't realize that you were on email.

A reply came back within a few minutes.

I wasn't until yesterday. I bought a computer and had a young fellow set it up and open an email account for me. You're the only person I felt comfortable sending my first message to. I'm very pleased it worked. Was prepared for failure.

Jack sat back and enjoyed an extraordinary burst of pride. Just then the computer gave out an odd beep. Then, a minute later, a second beep. Then a third.

In the meantime, for some reason there was nothing on the screen but a picture of spring flowers, and his bubble of pride burst when he realized that he had no idea how to get rid of all these flowers. He touched the mouse inadvertently and the flowers all vanished. There on the screen was his email inbox, containing the first four email messages he had ever received, three of them unread. It took only a few seconds for Jack to realize that the three messages were from his other drinking companions of a week previously. Jack sent polite one sentence replies to them.

Over the following three days, Jack received two further emails from Harry. One of these was a suggestion for a quick trip to The Factory at the end of Harry's working day. Jack accepted and they met.

They spent a very comfortable hour. It was strange for Jack, though, because Harry pulled from his jacket pocket a wad of typed pages and said that he had been reading Jack's paper.

"My paper? Which paper? How? I didn't send anything to you."

"No, I found it on Google."

"Where?"

"It's a tool that one can use to locate documents on the internet."

Jack's expression was one of complete confusion, so Harry passed him the document. Jack looked it over, then his face cleared.

"Oh. This is one of the papers I sent to Walter, the professor at University of Toronto who guides our informal discussion group. But how did you get this?"

After a longish discussion, Jack realized that he had probably been the only person sending stuff to Professor Reilly by regular mail, that the other five members of the group had been reading them on their computers.

"This is very interesting, Jack! But who was this fellow Owen Barfield?"

"Oh. He was a bit like me. No. I mean he was like me in that he was a lawyer who was interested in literature, but he accomplished some extraordinary things, whereas I have accomplished—"

"But what did he do? Let me step back a little, Jack. I have to say that what you have written here is full of … well … energy and youth. Could I read some of your other stuff sometime? But first, tell me a bit more about Barfield."

"Well, he lived an extraordinarily long and full life. He was educated at Oxford and he was ninety-nine when he died. He was a close associate of C.S. Lewis, who greatly admired him. He was a devout follower of Rudolf Steiner, and that's a problem for some people. He published quite a few books, the best one for me being *What Coleridge Thought*. That book caught a lot of academics napping. It's hard to classify him. He was an author, an extraordinary literary critic, a philosopher, and a sometime poet. The amazing thing about him is that he did a lot of his best work in his spare time."

Harry was gazing at Jack's paper, lost in thought, and several minutes passed. "Do you have any of Barfield's books?"

"I have them all."

They talked at length. But the discussion came in fragments, since Harry spent long minutes reading Jack's paper and thinking. Harry asked Jack many questions about his reading and his writing. For his part, Jack realized that he hadn't spoken so much at a single stretch for years, not even at Professor Reilly's monthly gatherings. And he found that he was more than a little flattered by Harry's questions and attention. They were both surprised when Harry glanced at his watch and did a double take.

"Good God! It's ten thirty! I had intended not to stay past eight thirty! I'm sorry to break off abruptly, Jack, but I have to get ready for a big meeting tomorrow. Will I see you at The Factory on Wednesday?"

"Oh. Yes."

Outside, they shook hands and Harry rushed off.

Wednesday rolled around quickly, and that evening the same group of men turned up at The Factory, occupied the same alcove, and had almost the same kind of wide-ranging discussion. Almost.

Jack surprised everyone by handing out business cards to them soon after he arrived. There was some interested discussion on this. Interested, but also surprised and impressed. Had Jack picked up a project, they wanted to know, and had that prompted him to have business cards printed, or was he just a sly old dog who tended to hide his light under a bushel?

"Oh. No. I just thought it would be a good idea to have some cards printed."

"Nice cards. Very good design", one of them commented.

"Oh. That was my nephew's work. He's a graphic artist."

The discussion was friendly and animated, as before. But Harry had been very quiet. Not that he said nothing, but he did a lot more listening this time than talking. Jack noted this, but put it down to one of the many vicissitudes of life, perhaps something that Harry was having to navigate at present. It would all settle down, come back to normal.

But it didn't.

At the next meeting at The Factory, Jack surprised them all much more by announcing that he had a Facebook page and handing out new business cards that included this information. There was a long discussion about this, and a lot of questions for Jack. In the end, Jack had a relatively simple and mild answer.

"Oh. It was something that I thought I should try. I decided it was time to become an intelligent dinosaur. There's not much I can do about being old and primitive. But at least I can be aware that asteroids exist and have some idea what to do if I see one coming."

This triggered another long discussion, in which Jack took part fairly freely. It was Harry who held back, looked from one to the other of them as they spoke. Considered. Reflected.

At subsequent Wednesday meetings, Jack spoke more. He asked questions. He even initiated some of the discussions. His appearance had also changed. His shirts were good-quality cotton. He wore name-brand jeans and well-shined leather slip-on shoes. At one of the meetings, several of the group noticed that when Jack entered The Factory, the barman said, "Hi Jack. All's well?", and there were waves of recognition from a few of the seated patrons.

It was a Saturday. Jack entered The Factory, and was met by several greetings, all of which were on the enthusiastic side of warm. Jack smiled and waved back. He had intended just to have a drink on his own. Walking straight to the bar, he greeted Ted, the barman, and ordered a pint of Tankhouse. When the pint had been drawn, Jack took a long sip of it, then turned to survey the room and its clientele. He reflected that he felt comfortable and at home, and this definitely would not have been his response just two months ago. Then he saw Harry.

Harry was seated on his own at a table off to the side of the room, a half-full glass of beer in front of him. He was in deep concentration over a book.

"Can I buy you another?"

Harry looked up in surprise, then smiled when he recognized Jack. "Hi Jack. Let me get them."

"Oh, no", Jack said as forcefully as he could, and turning to the bar he called out "Ted?" and made a sign indicating he wanted two more pints.

Harry invited him to sit down.

"I saw your postings on Facebook", Harry said. "All of them interesting."

"Oh. I thought that people might enjoy them."

They drank and talked a bit more.

"Good book?" Jack asked.

"Yes. Very."

Harry held up the book that had been lying on the table. It was a copy of *What Coleridge Thought*.

Jack felt a surge of pride and pleasure that he found impossible to explain.

Shelter

It was March. *And T.S. Eliot notwithstanding, March is pretty damn cruel as well,* thought Byrne. He owed that sentiment to one Angus McPhail, or more accurately, to his own reactions to the sod.

McPhail, an English teacher in Byrne's adolescence, a man feared and loathed during those high school classes in literature and composition, had been for some time an item long in the past. Nevertheless, for years McPhail had lived on in Byrne's memory as a whipping boy, lamentably only an abstract one, and the favoured mental voodoo doll target of Byrne's many pins of revenge. As today's cold March blast threw dust in his face, Byrne symbolically stuck in a couple more rusty pins. He took a moment to enjoy a self-satisfied smile at this, but paid for his inattention as his right foot landed awkwardly on an irregularity in the sidewalk. The electric arc of pain from an arthritic hip flashed through his leg and back, and Byrne thought viciously, *Shit! Can't even walk and stick McPhail at the same time!* As the pain ebbed away, Byrne mused sullenly that his voodoo doll had the wrong kind of mojo. It's McPhail who should be feeling the pain. But then the ominous reflection rose up before Byrne that maybe McPhail had his own voodoo doll as well.

It was Tuesday, the day he had agreed to meet Watson, the day they were to take their bus ride.

The bus ride had had an odd genesis, and as far as Byrne could recall, it began when he and Watson were enjoying a pint at The Keating Channel Pub.

"I'd like to go for a bus ride", Watson had said.

"Where?"

"Where? On the bus."

"Yes, I know, dickhead, but where to?"

Watson smiled. He knew Byrne's crusty manner and took no offence at it. In fact, he quite enjoyed Byrne's brusque comebacks, which were almost in direct contrast to his own mild statements.

"I've been thinking for some time" — and here he could sense various ripostes forming in Byrne's head ("Uh oh!" or "Danger ahead!" or "Here we go again!") — "thinking about just picking a city bus route and riding it to the end and back."

Byrne looked at him blankly. "What are you going to do at the end?"

"Nothing", Watson said, "just stay on the bus and ride back."

Byrne poked a bit more fun, until Watson said Byrne didn't need to come along if he didn't want to, and at that point Byrne held up his hands in surrender, because privately it was just quirky enough to appeal. So now here he was at the end station bus shelter waiting for the route 65 bus that would take them up Parliament Street to Castle Frank subway station and then back again, and there was Watson, pleasant, delightful, cheerful Watson, always presenting an infectious smile, always having a rolling confident gait, radiating his often irritating positive aura, now strolling toward him and the bus stop.

A few minutes later, the bus arrived, three people stepped out of it, and Byrne and Watson climbed on board, smiled at the pleasant young driver, flashed their seniors passes, and moved into the bus.

"Where do you want to sit?" Byrne asked.

"On the left-hand side."

"Why?"

"Because the bus goes near where I lived at one point, and I'll have a better view of that area from the left side of the bus."

No suitably caustic reply came to Byrne right away, so he chose a seat, stood aside to let Watson sit next to the window, then sat down himself and waited for the bus to move off. This didn't happen for about five minutes.

In the meantime, Byrne was amused to see Watson draw a notebook and pen from his pocket, turn to a fresh page, and in elaborate care, enter the date and the bus route.

"What are you doing?" Byrne asked.

"Getting ready to note anything of interest."

"What would be of interest?"

"Well, if I knew that, I'd already be noting it, wouldn't I?"

What an infuriating man, Byrne thought. And always that mild, civilized delivery. Why doesn't he ever get irritated, or better yet angry, or even better yet, boil over into a spleen-venting rant?

"I bet you have lots of those", Byrne said.

"Lots of what?"

"Lots of those notebooks. Been filling them for years, no doubt. Fifty or sixty of them piled up in a shoebox at home."

Watson said nothing, and the pause lengthened into a silence.

"Why are you taking notes?" Byrne asked, a note of ridicule trickling out through the words.

"Well, as you can see", Watson observed patiently, "I'm not taking notes. Not yet."

"Okay. When you will have completed your notes", Byrne articulated in exaggerated care, "what plans do you have for them? Will you hand them to the driver as suggestions on how he can do a better job? Will you use them as the basis for a long report to the TTC? Or is this in aid of some private project? Are you going to use them to write a masterpiece? *Remembrance of Bus Routes Past*? *The Bus Route in the Willows*? *The Old Man and the Bus Route*?"

"No, none of that", Watson said calmly. "I'm not really sure how I'll use my notes, or even whether I'll use them. But I realized a few weeks ago that I really don't know much about the city at all. I hit on this idea of riding buses to get a better picture. Where people work. Where they live. What their houses look like. What their streets look like. What their lives look like."

Byrne waited for Watson to continue.

"The idea of writing something is interesting, but I haven't really thought about it. Depends a bit, I guess, on what I see and what I note down. Maybe after I've ridden five or ten routes, there'll be something common, some interesting pattern, in my notes."

Just then, the driver closed the doors, the bus moved away from the stop, and they pulled into the Esplanade. Watson scanned out the windows on both sides of the bus in an eagerness that surprised Byrne.

"What do you hope to see?" Byrne asked, and was unable to keep the open curiosity out of his voice.

"I don't expect to see anything in particular, but I do expect to see things that I haven't noticed before, things that will make me wonder."

The bus made its first stop. Watson jotted two lines into his notebook, and looking down Byrne could read them as *Why Windmill?* and *Why Berkeley?*

"What do you mean *Why Windmill?*", Byrne asked.

"Do you know why that building on the right is called Windmill Co-operative? Or why this street is called Berkeley?"

"No."

"Nor do I. But I will find out."

The bus resumed its journey onto Berkeley Street, then turned right onto Front Street. Watson scanned the buildings passing on both sides. Byrne thought that Watson had the look, almost, of a young student on a school trip, and wondered to himself, *What put him onto this lark?*

The bus turned onto Parliament Street. Watson kept scanning out both sides of the bus.

"Aren't you going to note a question on why it's called Parliament Street?" Byrne queried, a bit peremptorily.

"No."

Byrne waited for more, but evidently more was not coming. *Why does he do this?*

"Okay. I'll bite. Why not?"

"Because I know why it's called Parliament Street."

The seconds trudged on, infuriatingly.

"For God's sake, do I have to drag everything out of you? Why is it called Parliament Street?"

"I'm not deliberately trying to annoy you", Watson began, "but I'm having to concentrate on what's passing outside. It's called Parliament Street because the first parliament in Upper Canada was located very near here."

"Really? Where?"

"Just back there, near the corner at Berkeley Street."

The bus moved on past Adelaide, Richmond. Byrne and Watson sat in companionable silence, while Watson made notes almost continuously. He moved onto a second page. Then onto a third. When Byrne glanced over, he saw notes like *Worts Lane, Factory/warehouse bldg (age?), terrace houses (Victorian? Edwardian?), community housing, shop fronts (once houses?), run down 2 blocks later gentrified (when? why?).*

The bus came to stop at lights, and Byrne asked, "Do you know why it's called Regent Park?"

Watson looked up. "Yes. There were two streets here when this housing was built. They were Regent Street and Park Street." The bus moved off and Watson bent over his notes again. He was now on the fifth page. *Carlton, not Carleton (why?), Amelia (who?), Wellesley (Arthur?), St Jamestown (tragic but what now?), why Necropolis?*

"Do you know who or what 'Bloor' was?" Byrne asked.

"Yes. A 'what'. He was a brewer."

The bus entered Castle Frank station and six passengers descended. The driver applied the parking air brake, said to them "End of the line, gentlemen", then he too left the bus.

"Probably needs a smoke", Byrne said.

"Or a whizz", countered Watson.

"Or a candy bar."

"Or to make a call to his wife."

"Or some fresh air."

"Or to listen to the birds."

"Or do some day-trading."

"Or stock up on toilet paper."

"Or just to get away from two old assholes talking nonsense."

They both laughed. Then Watson flicked through the notes he had made.

"Do you know why it's called 'Castle Frank' station?" Byrne asked, and the note of genuine curiosity in his voice caused Watson to look up.

"Yes. It's named after Simcoe's son Francis. Simcoe and Mrs. Simcoe had a sort of summer lodge over there near the edge of the valley, and it was from there, apparently, that Mrs. Simcoe watched the natives fishing at night by torchlight. It was a favourite spot for their young son Francis, so they called it Castle Frank. It was only a wooden structure, and my understanding is that it burnt down some years later. But by then, the Simcoes had moved back to England, John Simcoe had died, and Francis had joined the army. He was killed in the Peninsular Campaign under Wellington. Mrs. Simcoe lived well into the middle of the nineteenth century."

Byrne just sat there looking at Watson. He couldn't recall him ever uttering such a long speech. "Where did you learn all that?"

Watson shrugged. "Just picked it up."

"I didn't know you were interested in history."

"There's probably quite a bit about me that you don't know. We're not in the habit of having heart-to-heart chats."

They lapsed once again into companionable silence. In due course, the driver returned, nodded to them and said, "Gentlemen", and the bus began to retrace its route. Watson made another four pages of notes on the way back.

At the end stop, about fifty minutes later, they thanked the driver, descended from the bus, and shook hands.

"See you tomorrow?" Byrne half suggested, half asked.

"Yes. Where should we meet?"

"How about The Jason George?"

"Good", Watson replied. "At one o'clock."

They shook hands again and went their separate ways. As he walked away, Byrne realized idly that he had no idea where Watson lived.

Next day was cool and blustery, and The Jason George offered a welcome retreat from the weather. They followed their usual routine, which was to greet each other, ask how each was, inquire about anything new, order a pint, then find a quiet table and sit nursing their drinks during long periods of quiet company, punctuated by the occasional cryptic comment or question. Byrne was his harmlessly barbed self; Watson wore his conversational garb of mild observer; each seemed to the other to be inscrutably content.

"I enjoyed our bus ride yesterday", Byrne said neutrally.

"Yes. I plan to do another tomorrow, if you'd like to come along."

Byrne nodded past a mouthful of beer.

The next day, they did do another one, but it was a tram ride, the long Number 501, all the way out to the Neville Park loop, then to the Humber Loop at the other end and back again, more than an hour and a half one way. Watson took another fifteen pages of notes.

Over the following weeks, the process repeated itself. After refreshments in the spot that is, regrettably, no longer named The Stonecutter's Arms, in C'est What, in Scotland Yard, in The Beer Academy, in The Duke of Westminster, in The Beer Bistro, and a few others, the two of them rode the odd little Rosedale Bus, the Davenport Bus, the Chaplin-Glencairn Bus, the Cosburn Bus, the

Pape-Carlaw-Commissioners Bus, the Wellesley Bus, the St. Clair tram, the Dupont-Annette Bus, the St. Clair-Moore Avenue Bus, and six others. Although it was Byrne's impression that they spoke less and less during these rides, their silences seemed to be more and more companionable. During these weeks, Watson filled many notebooks. Byrne became increasingly curious, but in a fascinated rather than his standard mock-irritated or grumpy way. Byrne also reflected that although he didn't mind his own company, spending that much time with Watson was diverting in a peculiar way that caused him to reflect on the subtle differences between mild interest, quiet inactivity, and marginal but harmless boredom.

It was a bright, windless day, and small clouds dotted an impossibly blue sky. They were sitting in The Rebel House, out at the back under the parachute. They had just ridden the Avenue Road-Oriole Parkway Bus, Route 5.

"According to my count", Byrne began, "you have now filled twenty-seven notebooks on our bus rides."

"Twenty-nine", Watson corrected.

Byrne nodded. "What are you going to do with all those notes?"

"Well, I've spent quite a bit of time studying them. I have a far better picture of how people live in Toronto now."

"And that's it?" Byrne retorted, incredulously, impatiently.

"No. It caused me to remember and think seriously again of my studies long ago. One result is that I now look at things differently, I read the paper differently."

"Your studies?" Byrne barked. "What studies?"

"One of the things that you probably don't know about me is that I attended university."

"University? Where? When?"

"Here, in Toronto. Between the ages of eighteen and twenty-two."

"Here? I didn't know that! I didn't know there were universities back then! What did you study?"

"History and sociology."

"Well! I'll be damned!" Byrne exclaimed, after a longish pause. "So you got a degree! What did you do with it?"

Watson gazed into his beer for a long time before looking up at Byrne. "Just about nothing. That's the trouble."

"But what work did you do?"

"Oh! Nothing very exciting. I worked for years and years doing opinion surveys. I became quite good at it, and it paid fairly well. But, really, I wasted my time."

"How so?" Byrne asked.

"I became very interested in coming up with a definition and a measure of welfare — human welfare, that is, not welfare cheques — and then I became even more interested in the work of a man called Abraham Maslow. This didn't please my professors because they said that Maslow was barking up the wrong tree, and the academic judgment since then has been pretty much the same. But I think there was a lot of sour grapes to it."

Byrne struggled to get his head around all this, to link his quiet, modest, and unassuming drinking and verbal sparring partner to something that now seemed so, well, cosmic. Byrne stumbled and hunted for words. "Welfare? What? Tell me something about it."

"There's not much to tell. It all seemed to fizzle, in my view, because of a lot of pointless and egotistical academic hair-splitting. But it started off by people looking at five main things that could be used to develop a measure for a state of human welfare — food, shelter, clothing, education, and health care. I got interested in *shelter*, but it became obvious to me quite soon that these five are interrelated, and that they were influenced by external factors. So, for example, the requirements for some basic standard of shelter aren't the same in central Africa as they are in central Canada. The standards for food and for health care are probably fairly closely linked, at least in some ways."

Byrne appeared to be in a state of shocked interest. "Why did you become interested in all this again now?"

Watson took a drink of his beer and set down the glass. "Not too long ago, I read *The Joyless Economy* by a Hungarian-American economist, Tibor Scitovsky, who makes a case that culture comes down to being nothing more than a basic level of the knowledge that's needed to appreciate some larger reality, which might be art, music, literature, a set of mores or practices, or even another body of knowledge. I had never thought of that before, and it didn't take long for bits and pieces of my student project to start coming back to me."

Watson looked off into the distance.

"These five things — food, and the others — and what this guy — Maslow? — said, what happened to that?" Byrne asked.

Watson came back to the present and spread his hands in the standard sign of not knowing. "I hoped there could be some basis for agreeing on how to work back to something fundamental, and there was some very interesting debate on value."

"You mean the value of shelter?"

Watson shook his head. "Not *the* value. If one starts talking about *the* value of something, then the discussion gets derailed into that great swamp where value starts becoming confused with price and cost. Not the same things at all, and it takes one straight into the wasteland that Oscar Wilde foresaw."

"What? Who? Oscar who?"

"Wilde", Watson explained patiently. "He was the guy who accused people in the late nineteenth century of knowing the price of everything and the value of nothing. If only he could see us now! He was at least a hundred years ahead of his time."

"I'm not sure I…", Byrne began, then faded off into uncertainty.

Watson nodded in understanding. "Stop me if what I'm saying is too simple", he said. "You can think of value as that essence that causes people to regard something as important in its own right. If one tries to strip something of any sense of monetary or exchange worth that attaches to it, and this is pretty much impossible at one level, then maybe one can begin to distinguish between needs and wants. That's the line of thinking I was pursuing back then. Nowadays, it's much harder because advertising has become a massive and central element of modern life. Advertisers are very keen to create wants but then to convince people that those wants really are needs."

"So what happened?" Byrne asked.

"You mean what happened to the whole effort or to my student project?"

"The whole effort."

"Well, basically it turned out that there was no way of reaching any agreement on a baseline. Maslow defined what he called a hierarchy of needs, the lowest one being what had to be met in order to insure just sheer brute survival, the highest one being self-actualization. I was trying to find a way to put these together, but my profs did everything they could to discourage me. The academics did what academics do; they argued, split hairs, pissed about until everyone was exhausted."

It was as though Watson had just pulled off a mask and revealed a total stranger.

"So what happened?" Byrne asked.

"Nothing. I finished my final-year project, everyone liked it, I got a very good mark for it, but privately they all told me it was a dead end. Reading Scitovsky revived my old interest in the notion of shelter, and I began wondering about how people live here — and that gave me the idea of riding around on buses to have a look. Now I wish that back then I had told them all to get lost and found some way to carry on. But…"

Byrne asked more questions until their glasses were empty. Watson looked at his watch. "I'd like to visit the library before it closes" — and they both paid, got up, and left.

They walked down Yonge Street, heading for the crossing that would lead them to the Rosedale subway station. They stopped to wait for the light to change, standing next to the shelter for the Yonge Street bus.

A young woman approached them. She was wearing photo ID on a lanyard and asked if they had a few minutes. She wanted to take a photo of them for her media studies project at Ryerson. Byrne and Watson both nodded pleasantly because she had an attractive smile, and these days discussions with young women were rare occurrences that one didn't turn down.

She arranged them the way she wanted, took about a dozen pictures, asking them to adjust their positions and their facial expressions every few minutes.

"Thank you very much, gentlemen", she said through a brilliant smile.

She began turning to move away, when Watson said "Excuse me, miss, if you don't mind me saying 'miss'."

She turned back to them, smile just as bright, but a questioning eyebrow now inviting Watson to continue.

"Could we possibly get copies of some of those pictures?"

"Oh, yes, certainly! Just give me your—" But then she stopped. Much later, Watson realized that she was probably going to ask them for an email address, but then said to herself that they likely didn't have such a thing, and possibly not even a computer.

She looked around. "Over there", she said. "It says they have a copy centre." Then she pulled something out of the large handbag she was carrying, fiddled with her camera, then did a bit more fiddling. Almost immediately, the pictures she had taken scrolled across a small screen. "Which ones would you like?"

"They're all good", Watson said in obvious admiration at her skill. "How about that one, that one, and um, that one?"

"Good. Let's go", she said, and struck out across the street.

Within three minutes, they each had large utility prints of three pictures. The girl handed Watson a small object made of metal and plastic.

"It's a flash drive. All the pictures are on there. If you take this into any Staples, they'll help you print out other pictures you want." She hesitated a moment, then in a returning flush of enthusiasm, said, "Thanks! You two guys are lovely" and she strode off up Yonge Street, looking for her next target.

Watson opened the folder that contained his three pictures. They looked at the pictures, looked at each other, and smiled. Gazing back at them were images of two elderly gents, wispy white hair on the left, thinning but tight and wiry salt-and-pepper on the right, sunlight angling across their smiling faces.

In the background was a bus shelter.

Paying Debts

Nobody recognized him. Very few people even noticed him, which was odd since strangers were almost always noticed.

One couldn't call him arresting or attractive. In no way was he either charismatic or memorable. At least, not right away.

He was of medium height, had a long but faint scar on his left cheek, had shortish light-brown hair, grey eyes, and walked with a slight limp. He held his left arm across his abdomen, making it impossible to see right away that the arm was partially withered. His clothes were clean and well kept. He looked like an itinerant farm labourer, several of whom passed through the town every month in the summer. A small leather bag was slung over one shoulder, and the several tied thongs indicated that the bag had multiple pockets, a large one, probably for a few spare clothes, and two smaller ones, one of which appeared to contain a small amount of food.

In the centre of the town there was a well, and he stopped there, asked politely whether he might have a drink of water, and when he received a nod of agreement he pulled a small mug from his shoulder bag.

Two other men stood leaning against the well. The quality and cut of their clothes, their well-made and polished shoes, their grooming in general, and their slight corpulence, all spoke of men who were financially secure.

"You looking for work?" one of them asked the newcomer after a longish silence and an equal period of open and frank assessment.

The newcomer smiled. "I'm always interested in doing some work."

"What can you do?"

"I'm good at carpentry, also at wood carving. I can work with leather. For some years I was a potter. And I can work fields — tilling, sowing, harvesting."

The larger and more imposing of the two prosperous men looked over the newcomer more closely and nodded once.

"Come over to my shop" — and he pointed across the street — "this afternoon. I know people who might be able to use you."

"Thank you kindly", the newcomer replied, dipping his mug into the bucket and taking another long drink of water. "Yes. Thank you kindly, sir."

The prosperous man began to turn away, but then stopped, faced the newcomer once more, and asked his name.

"People call me Piper, sir. Just Piper."

And that was how it all started.

The newcomer stood by the well for another few moments, then went off to take a look at the town.

He had come from the south, along the route that became the main thoroughfare, wound through the main part of the town, and gradually rose toward a large hill lying to the north. The top of the hill was covered by a thick beech forest, and cattle grazed on the steep grassy portion of the hill just below the line where the beech forest began. The main thoroughfare split into two less imposing tracks that diverged to either side of the hill. A stream flowed alongside each of these two tracks and then joined in a stone channel that followed the left side of the main thoroughfare. At the point where the main thoroughfare emerged from the southern edge of the town, the stream flowed into a pond held behind a small dam. Next to this dam was a mill, and on the other side of the thoroughfare, which at about that point became once more just a track, there was a smithy, a tannery, and a small shambles.

He had noticed all this on his way in, so he carried on toward the north, noting the rich bottomland extending to the east, the well-maintained stone wall that stretched off to the east, the rich crops, the people out working the fields, the unworked grassland, the few small crudely enclosed vegetable plots, a scruffy orchard, and a handful of emaciated cattle grazing in the tall grass.

Continuing to round the large promontory presented by the hill, the newcomer was somewhat surprised to come upon what looked like another village, less than a few minutes' walk from the attractive town he had just left. The houses in this village were small and mean. He was soon to learn that a similar settlement crowded around the track that skirted the other side of the headland hill. In fact, these weren't separate villages, as he had supposed initially. They were the poor sections of the town whose prosperous area he had just left.

The newcomer walked through the few streets and laneways as existed. Some of the houses were little better than lean-to structures, and even the best of the dwellings were just unsatisfactory patchworks of many overlapping and ad hoc repairs. The people looked under-nourished, there were no real smiles, and their eyes signalled the hopelessness that they evidently felt. But they were kind and civil to him, saying hello, and returning his greetings. A few chickens pecked fecklessly at the dry earth. Behind one row of houses, a couple of pigs slept in the sun. Some women washed clothes by hand and three unshod and none-too-clean children ran down the street and vanished behind a tumbledown building that might have been a barn at one time.

When the newcomer judged it to be early afternoon, he returned to the prosperous section of the town, entered the shop that had been pointed out to him, and immediately recognized the prosperous man.

"Ah, my good fellow. Do come in. Over here, if you don't mind", and the newcomer was led to a corner of the shop that was screened from the view of regular customers. "I have here a list of three gentlemen who could use your skills", and he handed the newcomer a small piece of paper, his face seeming to bear an odd, slightly superior, almost mocking expression. The newcomer looked the list over quickly, then directed his gaze at the prosperous man.

"And where can I find these men, ah, Mr. Treadwell, Mr. Black, and Mr. Furnival?"

The prosperous man's expression had changed to one of surprise.

"Yes", the newcomer said and flashed a brilliant smile. "People do sometimes have trouble believing that I can read."

"I presume, sir, that you are able to write as well?" the prosperous man ventured, now openly curious.

Without saying a word, the newcomer took the quill from the prosperous man's table, turned over the piece of paper he had just been given, and in an elegant flowing hand, he wrote out the first verse from the Book of Ecclesiastes.

Within ten minutes, the newcomer had agreed to spend one day a week working for the prosperous man.

Barely three weeks later, stories about the newcomer were on the lips of everyone within the prosperous part of the town. He was asked to open a school. He was in demand from every business in the town, and the prosperous man made it clear that he had locked down his one day a week for the foreseeable future.

He had done work for Treadwell, Black, and Furnival, and the quality of his work had become a matter of general acknowledgement.

But the newcomer had also spent a good deal of time in the poor sections of the town. He spoke to quite a few people, and helped two of them modify their houses and revamp and enlarge their gardens. The impact on the properties was small, barely detectable unless one looked closely. But the greater impacts lay elsewhere.

Life was just as hard. The work was just as back-breaking. The recompense was just as meagre. But on the faces of those the newcomer had spent time with, there was a new impulse to smile, an increase in self-confidence, and a greatly spiked interest in doing more. A further six weeks passed, and the mood of the poor sections of the town had changed. This change began to be spoken about in the prosperous regions, and the newcomer decided it was time to take a broader initiative.

The prosperous man the newcomer had met initially was all smiles by this time. His business was booming, and his face glowed in benevolent self-satisfaction. Had it not been him, after all, who had taken the first initiative? Had it not been as a result of his arrangement with the newcomer that the rest of the prosperous part of the town was benefitting?

It was on a bright sunny day, when the prosperous man's mood seemed to be at its apex, that the newcomer made his suggestions. For only modest considerations, he had explained, the fortunes of everyone in the town, whether prosperous or impoverished, could be raised. There would be more trade. The tithe barn would be full to brimming. And with only a little luck, the need for alms might vanish altogether.

Such was the currency of the newcomer that only a few people questioned his proposals, and they were soon drowned out by the large majority. There was just one condition.

"I am working as many hours as the Lord sends, but am being paid for only a few of those. What I'm suggesting will greatly benefit the commonweal, and for my efforts I ask only to be compensated reasonably."

A general objection was soon raised.

"But that would mean that we, here in this part of our town, would need to pay so that they, those people over in that part of the town, can benefit."

"Everybody will benefit", the newcomer explained calmly, "although it is true that initially the poor will benefit most. But their need and your resources are both greater."

It didn't rest easily. Many people were reluctant to agree. Most were disgruntled that things had taken this turn. And that situation likely would not have changed, had the rumour not spread.

The newcomer is thinking of moving on.

From that point, discussions took on a more serious face, and an agreement was eventually reached.

The newcomer would be paid one tenth of what he had requested until the value of his proposal became evident, and the end of the harvest was chosen as the time at which that judgment would be made. If all were sufficiently satisfied, the newcomer would then be paid the remaining nine-tenths of his money as a lump sum.

From that moment on, a new mood overcame the place, dwarfing the sense of expectancy that had arisen until then. The newcomer seemed to be everywhere. His brilliant smile beamed, his eyes flashed, and his advice and encouragement covered the poor section of the town like a protective blanket. He trained all and sundry in the arts of carpentry, and soon a few of the hovels in the poor section of town rose to the level of the modestly well-kept places in the prosperous part of the town. The newcomer appeared to be inexhaustible. He demonstrated how to do things, he encouraged, he suggested improvements, new departures, upgrades. Garden plots expanded massively. Proper hen houses were erected. Pig sties were built.

As summer came toward its end, the land yielded previously unknown quantities of fruit and vegetables. Children and adults alike glowed in the health that an ample diet, a better diet, produced. And relations between those in the poor and prosperous parts of the town displayed something that had been unknown before: the first signs of goodwill.

The harvest began in earnest. The bounty that the newcomer had helped the people coax from Nature was beyond their experience. Granaries were full and overfull. The tasks of laying down various foodstuffs for use over the winter, once so depressing because the pitifully small amounts of produce took so little time to deal with, now demanded all the people's spare energy because of the superabundance of the harvest. They all worked late into the nights, the newcomer being there among them, smiling, laughing in genuine pleasure at their happiness, encouraging them on.

And then it was done.

The poor people staged their own harvest festival, the first one they had ever even been able to conceive of, and although they tried to make the newcomer the star of the show, he refused to accept that accolade.

"You have done this, you yourselves!" he declared. "I have just given you advice here and there. This is something you can now do for yourselves every year."

There was great rejoicing. Though the poor people now had newfound and strong confidence, privately they all knew that the newcomer had driven poverty and hunger from their midst.

The newcomer moved confidently among all the people in the town, the poor people especially, but also the prosperous people. Three days after the harvest festival staged by the poor people, he asked the prosperous man, for whom he still worked one day a week, to arrange for the town to settle his account, to pay him the remaining nine-tenths as they had agreed.

Nothing happened for almost a week.

The newcomer approached the prosperous man once more.

"Ah, yes!" the man boomed, his face a picture of bonhomie. "There has been a-a change, yes, a change."

"A change?"

"Yes. We have discussed the matter a great deal. Please be aware that we are very grateful indeed for what you have helped us accomplish. Very grateful indeed."

There was a pause here. The newcomer waited patiently.

"We have agreed, and please know that this was only after a great amount of reflection and consideration, we have agreed, ah, that value has been delivered both ways. We do want to thank you most sincerely."

"You have decided not to pay me what you agreed, what you owe me. Is that it?"

"My good man, that is putting matters rather bluntly—"

"But that's about the size of things, is it?"

"Er, ah, yes. I'm afraid it is."

The newcomer smiled pleasantly.

"Then, sir, I will be leaving your lovely town tomorrow at first light."

"But" — the prosperous man began, a look of alarm on his face at being about to lose such a valuable resource — "but you are most welcome to stay, most welcome indeed. I personally would be delighted to have you work for me two days a week. And at an increased rate of pay."

"Very generous of you sir, and thank you for the offer. But it really is time for me to move on."

They spoke for a few more minutes, the prosperous man extended his hand and gave a warm handshake.

And then the newcomer was gone.

News spread through the town overnight and during the next morning like a brush fire.

The people, both prosperous and poor, were in a state of disbelief all day.

That evening, just after sunset, the first cries and wails of agony were heard in the prosperous part of town…

This story was inspired by the tale of the Pied Piper of Hamelin.

The Walnut Shell

My trip to Germany was extended because of a broken leg. As originally planned, it would be eight long and stressful days, so why not tack on a few more days and season it with a bit of energetic relaxation?

The first five days involved a predictable but exhausting hunt through four German cities looking for machine components for two Canadian clients. I found German businessmen to be, in general, a no-nonsense crowd. They appreciated people who knew exactly what they wanted, although they pushed back when challenged on details of their products or costs. I pushed pretty hard. They pushed back. After some manoeuvring I concluded the discussion.

"I'll speak to my client and finalize an order tomorrow", I said in the end. I did. And we did.

One down.

My second commission for the trip, a business excursion to the Frankfurt Book Fair, was now up to bat. Seven years in technical editing had taken me to a number of gatherings where technical literature was front and centre, and in that past life, I had been to the Frankfurt Book Fair once. My hugely competitive friend, Leo Goldstein, had fallen heavily on the tennis court and broken his right humerus, and it was that event that had put me in Leo's sights to attend the Book Fair on his behalf. I started off firmly decided that I would say no to Leo.

"They wanted a colleague to take my place", he had said to me, in that tone of mild outrage at the pool of idiocy that lapped all around him. "I told them no. It has to be McCracken. So do it for me, Doug."

He had settled this in his own mind long before any mention was made to me.

"What's wrong with your colleague?" I asked, not really wanting to take on the extra task.

"Apart from just about everything, he doesn't know his ass from his hair parting. You, on the other hand, you can do this in your sleep. Your German is as close as dammit to being fluent."

"Well, I've got a full slate already", I lied shamefully.

"Come on, Doug! Do I have to say pretty please? Offer you a year's worth of Versace underwear? Okay. Let me say that I'll make it worth your while."

"How?"

"Well, you name it."

Goldstein is one stubborn bugger, and he could easily drag this out for another half hour. I thought hard and fast.

"All right. Buy me a three-day bicycle trip along the lower Main valley." There were many choices, but I recalled an earlier bicycle trip along the bike paths that followed this river.

Leo brought his hands together, as though shaking on a deal he had made with himself. But his expression indicated his puzzlement at anyone wanting to do something so ridiculous.

"That's my man!" he said past his huge infectious smile. "Book it and send me the bill!"

So, after three days at the book fair, more than a dozen back and forth SMS exchanges, and having placed book orders worth slightly more than $4000, I found myself in the lovely town of Lohr, adjusting the saddle of a newish e-bike. It was the start of the first day of a three-day jaunt that would end in Aschaffenburg, just up the Main from Frankfurt. By eight thirty, I was pedalling down the superb bike path, the Main drifting idly to my right. A lone heron flew past in welcome.

Mixed forest on the hills surrounding the Main soon gave way to rows of vines that climbed with Teutonic energy up, high up, on slopes rising from the river. It was clear that those slopes had been chosen by eyes that were discerning. Delicate sweeping brush strokes of cirrus decorated an otherwise cloudless sky. Passing the first small village, I cycled through invisible scents of breakfasts being prepared. Within a half hour, I had set a decent pace, and the world of books and machine tools had become as distant and irrelevant as the far side of the moon.

There were pleasant greetings of "Morgen" from some of the cyclists travelling in the other direction, and after an hour and a half, I stopped at a picnic table sitting by the bike path, watched a Main barge manoeuvre its way into a lock, and sipped contentedly from my water bottle. A couple I judged to be in their late sixties pulled off the bike path, parked their bikes, and joined me at the table. There was the usual "Good morning" and "Where are you headed today", and I guessed from their accents that they were probably from Berlin or somewhere near it.

When I'm in Germany, I always try to speak in an accent as close as possible to that of the several German instructors I have had over the years, all of whom have come from Aachen for some odd reason. And although perfection seems to be impossible, I try to make the guessing game of my German interlocutors as difficult as I can.

"Sind Sie Englisch?" the woman asked, openly intrigued.

"Not English. Canadian", I replied in German.

Their response to the news that I was Canadian reflected a combination of surprise and delight that I always found charming and complimentary. I got them talking about Berlin, they chatted happily for about five minutes, then water bottles were stowed and we set off again separately.

The sun climbed into the sky, more villages and their beautifully maintained buildings floated past, and I crossed the Main at the next major town. There was a break for some lunch at a patio overlooking the river, and while a sausage and some wine warmed the inner man, the body basked in the heat of the day. Setting off again, the remaining fifteen kilometres led me past four impossibly lovely villages, and eventually I drew up outside my hotel at the end of the first day. A shower, a change of clothes, a nap, and a large glass of Pilsener set me up for an excellent meal of sauerbraten, consumed slowly in the hotel's attractive beer garden. The day's exercise, sunshine, fresh air, and ever changing surroundings had placed me firmly in Radlerland, a cyclist's heaven. I was fast asleep by nine thirty.

Apart from my work, which delivers considerable satisfaction at the cost of being quite demanding, my life back home was very full. Full of activities and full of friends. It didn't hurt that I don't mind my own company. But as I awoke the next morning, all of that felt far removed. A quick shave and one of those German breakfasts that can see off the wolf until mid-afternoon seemed to be the appropriate precursor to climbing back onto the saddle. As on the day before, most people on the bike path seemed to be in pairs. I considered idly what it would be like to cycle with a companion.

This second day was a repeat of the first, but after finding my hotel, having a quick shower and change of clothes, I found a spot just along the river where a group of tables offered a sweeping display of vines that carpeted the bend on the opposite side of the river. Back at the hotel, a half litre of Bitburger found a welcome home, after which I opted for a blowout meal of *Schweinshaxe*.

At breakfast the next morning, I was all too aware that my last day of cycling was about to begin. Although I would spend that night at Aschaffenburg before returning to Frankfurt and my flight home, I determined to extract value from every minute. Parking my room key, and thereby claiming a table next to a row of windows, I went to survey the food laid out along one end of the breakfast room. It was varied, appealing, and generous. I collected a poppy seed roll, a hard-boiled egg, a large chunk of Montagnolo, a couple of sausages, and an assortment of vegetables. Turning to fill a glass with apricot juice, I bumped lightly into someone.

"Oh! Entschuldigung!" she said.

"Nein! Schuld habe ich", I replied.

We smiled, moved apart, and made our way to our separate tables. My breakfast was slow and relaxed.

But in the end, getting back on my bike was something of a priority because there was quite a bit to see in Aschaffenburg. I picked up my key from the table and gazed idly around the room, which was quite busy by then, but my gaze stopped at the woman with whom I had collided twenty minutes earlier. She was three tables away, and I realized that she was also in cycling gear. She mouthed a wish for a good day on the bike path and sent me a smile that was friendly and natural. I smiled back, rose, and left.

The day's cycling was just as fresh and appealing as that of the previous two days. The weather was fine and clear. There was no wind. The scenery was gorgeous. But as happens toward the end of a trip, the problems and concerns that I had carefully parked earlier now crept back to tap insistently at my mind's door. I ignored them as well as I could and just spent the day living in the moment.

At the hotel in Aschaffenburg, I turned in the bicycle, showered, changed, and set out to see what I could of the city in the time available. At six o'clock, I went down to defeat, having seen only a fraction of the things on my list. Back at the hotel, the beer garden called to me and was the obvious place to have dinner. Choosing a table near the trunk of a giant walnut tree, I accepted the menu from the waiter with a smile and asked for a glass of Müller-Thurgau. The wine arrived, I sipped it appreciatively, decided on a Jägerschnitzel, and then spent a moment looking around the beer garden.

My walnut tree dominated the space, and the afternoon sun filtered down through the leaves, which seemed to glow above me in multiple hues of green. Flowers in pots of various sizes graced the garden at irregular locations, some nestled among the vines that festooned the wooden fence, some on the ground, and some on poles placed among the tables. There was one large table, the sign *Stammtisch* on it reserving it in perpetuity for use only by locals. About fifteen other tables were dotted around the garden. I sipped more wine, completed my appreciation of the beer garden, and just then the woman from breakfast stepped through the pergola doorway and stopped to choose a place to sit. I set down my glass and rose.

"Would you like to join me for dinner?" I asked in German.

"Yes. I would like that", she said without hesitation, in English.

So much for my presumed competence in German.

She walked over to my small square table, chose the seat to my left, and we sat. Her eye caught the waiter.

"I didn't mean to imply that my English is better than your German, and I'm sorry if it sounded like that", she said, as if reading my thought. Her English was indeed almost perfect mid-Atlantic, just a slight hint of something suggesting maybe a Dutch or Nordic origin.

"My name is Britta", she offered, probably ruling out Holland.

"Doug", I replied. "Doug McCracken."

The waiter approached our table, and she ordered that mixture of dry white wine and soda water that is often called a spritzer in North America, but is usually a *Schorle* in Germany.

"Where did you start this trip?" I asked.

"Bamberg."

"Long way."

"Yes. But very nice scenery. And you?"

"I'm doing a short version. From Lohr. Squeezed in at the end of a business trip and the need to get back home again."

"Where's home?" she asked.

"Toronto", I replied, apparently somewhat diffidently.

She smiled. "No need to be apologetic about it. I was there two years ago. Enjoyed it very much."

"It's not a question of being apologetic", I said. "I just get very tired of things being oversold." Wanting to change the subject, I asked, "What do you do for a living?"

"Oversold", she said, offering a speculative look. "Interesting."

We sipped.

"I'm a translator", she said.

"And do you work in — I'm guessing — Denmark? Or…"

"Very good guess", she said. "I am Danish but I work in Berlin."

The waiter appeared to be hovering, so Britta opened her menu and began studying it. I took the opportunity to look at her more closely now, supplementing impressions made as she walked toward the table.

She appeared to be about my own age, early forties, but clearly took care of herself. Her light sandy hair was cut to medium length and she wore the merest hint of make-up that gave her grey-blue eyes a stunning presence. It appeared that she made no effort to hide the small scar on the left side of her chin. Her build was slight, she was about 175 centimetres in height (or about five feet nine inches as I would have said years ago), and she was wearing brown flat shoes, pale-blue good quality jeans, and a cream cotton top.

The waiter approached our table, and Britta ordered a *Wurstsalat* plate.

"I'll have a green salad with that if it doesn't come with one", she said to the waiter. Her German was impeccable, but once again having that tone in some of the vowels. She turned to me. "Where did you learn such good German?" she asked, but then a cloud passed behind her eyes. "There I go again!" she said, in self-reproach.

"No", I insisted. "Not at all. Too many North Americans who travel don't speak anything other than English. You ask a fair question. I worked at one point for a German subsidiary in Canada. I've always liked languages. A chance came to work in Germany and I took it. I assume almost everybody in Denmark speaks some German."

"Yes, I guess so", she said, after a pause.

We settled into a set of questions and answers on what we do, and it soon became clear that we were both absorbed in our work.

Our meals arrived, and conversation became punctuated by longish periods of eating. The waiter came by to check that everything was okay. We both nodded, and I pointed to Britta's almost empty glass.

"Another?" I asked her in German.

"Ja. Du auch?"

"Ja. Ich auch."

The waiter returned with two glasses on a tray, deposited them, and went away again. We soon finished our meals. I wiped my mouth on my napkin, leaned back slightly, and smiled across at Britta. But before I could phrase another question, a clattering above us signalled the descent of what sounded like several walnuts. Four of them, all in their green coverings, landed at various spots around our table. One rolled close to my right foot. I looked down and noticed another already lying there but without its green covering. I picked it up. When I squeezed the light tan shell, the two halves moved slightly. I forced my thumbnails between and slowly pulled. Inside were two perfect half walnuts. Carefully removing the flimsy internal partitions, I managed to extract the two intact halves.

I passed one to Britta. "Do have a walnut."

She laughed. "If we were in a men's club, it would probably be 'Do have a cigar'."

"Yes. Probably", I said. "Although I know nothing about men's clubs."

"Really? I half expected you to belong to several."

"I do, of course. But it's not the done thing to flaunt those facts. But do share this walnut."

We ate the walnut halves.

"Since I've been to Toronto", Britta began, "I suppose I should ask whether you've been to Berlin."

"Yes. Many years ago. But I'm due for another visit. There's so much of interest in Berlin."

We both nodded.

"Is this trip just a break for you or does it involve something else?" I asked.

She shook her head. "Just a break. Although I do a lot of cycling in Berlin also. No need for a car. But cycling in the countryside is a nice change."

We talked some more. She asked what I meant specifically when I said there was so much of interest in Berlin. I explained about the hooks in my technical background that lead to many of the great German physicists of the nineteenth and early twentieth centuries.

"Physicists? Who, for example?"

"Well the great example for me is Max Planck, and it's a real tragedy that his house and all his private papers were destroyed during the war. But not just physicists. Lots of mathematicians too. It all harks back to the time when Germany was top of the heap in so many fields."

"Sounds like any visit you make to Berlin would need to be a long one." We signalled the waiter, he came over, and we went through the ritual of paying.

Change was pocketed. She collected her handbag. The evening was changing key.

"That was an excellent meal", Britta said, with some feeling.

"Indeed. Excellent." Having tied the ribbons on our meal, I looked at her and our eyes met.

"I have some schnapps", I offered, "if you'd like an after dinner drink."

She smiled.

"So do I", she said, matching my move. "Some very good Italian peach brandy."

We looked at each other for a long moment. Britta's hand closed on her room key resting on the table. I smiled and raised an eyebrow. She smiled back, and we rose and left together.

Even before we reached her room, our defences were dismantled and set to one side. She closed the door behind us, I drew her to me gently and kissed her on the neck. Language was no longer needed.

For me, there is something about the first button being undone. There begins to be revealed then the great power somehow associated with that mysterious and compelling sexual divide that men and women gaze across from opposite sides. It can be an insuperable barrier, a chasm across which we try to connect. But occasionally one also finds a bridge.

That night it was a bridge.

On that bridge, physical contact opened the way for us to whimsy, laughter, and discussion. We talked. About Copenhagen, Berlin, Toronto. About music and literature. About food and wine. It felt as though I had known her for years.

Three long and intimate meetings on the bridge punctuated that conversation, leaving us both with those faint smiles that reflected sated desire, but also signalled the arrival of the endorphins that had come to whisper us to sleep.

I awoke at three thirty.

Her back, shifting slowly to the rhythms of her deep and steady breathing, glowed faintly in the night light next to the bathroom door. I slipped quietly from her bed, collected my clothes and shoes, and risked a short walk in the buff to my own room down the hall.

Next morning, showered, shaved, dressed, packed, and ready to catch a reasonably early train to Frankfurt, I descended to the breakfast room.

"Has the lady from room twelve come to breakfast yet?" I asked the young man who seemed to be in charge of breakfast operations, and who had just taken my order for coffee. He consulted his checklist.

"Yes. She was here quite early and has eaten and left."

I selected what I wanted for breakfast, returned to my table, and sat, but immediately rose again. Reaching into the back pocket of my jeans, I pulled out the two half shells of a walnut. I didn't remember doing so, but I must have scooped them off the table as we left the beer garden.

They were perfectly formed, and together were a work of art, inside and out.

The walnut meat was gone.

But the shell endured.

It recalled a memory of the bridge where human meaning can be found, sometimes transient, sometimes lasting, always important, always to be sought. I looked again at the two half shells and saw what had been and what could be again.

Sand Trap

"Have you heard?"

This was a question blurted out by Dorothy. It was a straightforward question, expressed in an urgency indicating something serious, but it also had that undertone of illicit excitement.

A number of ladies waited expectantly for her reply. Mrs. Parr gave them her trademark look, an expression that managed, at the same time, to signal open and curious interest, but also the threat of a quick, piercing, and deflationary response if the load of idiocies already placed upon her by a vague and unthinking world was about to be increased.

"Heard?" she asked. "Heard what?"

Looks passed quickly among the ladies. Pamela Davidson, a long time member of the club, and perhaps the most pragmatic, forthright, and no-nonsense individual, grasped the nettle.

"The greenskeeper found a man's body this morning."

"A man's body", Mrs. Parr repeated without any particular emphasis or hint of a double take.

"Yes. William found it about half an hour ago. He called the police", and almost as if on cue, a siren wailed briefly out at the main road, demanding passage. There was the sound of a car accelerating, and it quickly appeared rounding the slope just to the west of the clubhouse. The car stopped next to a greenskeeper, there was a brief conversation through an open window, the greenskeeper climbed in the back seat, and the car once more rushed onward, even before the door had closed. They turned past the clubhouse at speed, stopped in front of the maintenance building, and then quickly all climbed into a golf cart. William drove them in the cart out onto the course.

Mrs. Parr didn't mention that after he had made his discovery William had contacted her right away, she being the senior person present, had told her all the details, and she had asked him to tell nobody and to contact the police immediately. But she was amazed once more at how quickly news could leak out.

Several of the ladies looked at Mrs. Parr, who was considered generally to be the éminence grise at the club, in almost every respect.

"Well, I'm going inside", Mrs. Parr said quietly and began to turn toward the members' lounge.

"But what about the body?" one of the ladies asked.

"I'm afraid I can't do anything about that", Mrs. Parr replied, hiding her internal agitation that something this horrible could have occurred here. "I came here for an early round of golf. The course has been closed now, so I'm not able to do that. It is possible to have an early drink, so I plan to do that instead."

"But shouldn't we wait for them?" another member said plaintively.

"Wait for who?" someone responded.

"Well … the police … I mean…"

"The police are already doing their job", Pamela said. "Mrs. Parr is right. There's no advantage to waiting out here."

"But won't they want to question us?" This from another member.

"Probably. But they'll be able to find us."

"This is outrageous! This is the Upper Canada Ladies' Golf Club!" The speaker was a slim tanned woman of about sixty-five who seemed to wear a slight but permanent scowl. She was known only as Mrs. Wrigley.

Pamela gave Mrs. Wrigley a hard stare. "By all accounts, a human being is dead. Granted, this isn't a slum area, nor is it frequented by mobsters, as far as we know. But a little compassion seems in order, until we find out just what happened."

There were murmurs of assent, and they all moved slowly toward the members' lounge.

Pamela made her way toward the bar where Mrs. Parr was already standing, sipping a glass of tonic water and ice, and asked for the same.

"Dreadful! Absolutely dreadful!" Mrs. Parr said quietly.

"Indeed it is, Louise." Pamela was one of the few people who felt comfortable addressing Mrs. Parr by her given name. "I suppose the police will want to interview us."

"Probably", Mrs. Parr responded.

"But surely that will be just a formality."

"Well", Mrs. Parr began, turning to look at Pamela, "if what we're told is true, there is a body on our golf course."

"But surely you don't think—"

"I don't think anything, Pamela. We will just need to wait and see."

"But it could hardly be that any of our members—"

"I don't mean to keep interrupting you Pamela, but we do need to keep open minds, and we just need to wait. At this point, we don't know anything."

"No. You're right. We'll probably learn something from William when he returns."

"I doubt that. The police are most likely collecting evidence. They won't want people discussing it and speculating, filling in gaps in their own stories."

The two ladies finished their tonic and ice, and ordered seconds. Mrs. Parr looked around the twenty or so women in the lounge. She knew them all. Had known them all for years. They were all intelligent and all were good golfers. With only the rare exception, they were pleasant, decent human beings, and now that the initial impact of the news had worn off, their expressions signalled concern, and compassion for whoever it was whose body lay out there.

About forty-five minutes after they had collected in the members' lounge, a policewoman entered the room. She had short black hair, was in her mid to late thirties, and wore comfortable, summer, business attire.

"Could I have your attention please. I'm Detective Constable Helen Campbell. I'm going to need your time. I'll be speaking to all of you. I want to begin with Mrs. Parr and Mrs. Davidson."

Louise Parr and Pamela Davidson set down their drinks and went over to identify themselves.

DC Campbell introduced herself formally to the two ladies, said that it didn't matter which of them was interviewed first, and that she expected all this to be just a formality. Pamela and Mrs. Parr looked at each other, Mrs. Parr offered a "you first" sign, and Pamela and the DC went into the dining room. Fifteen minutes later, Campbell stuck her head around the dining room door and gestured to Mrs. Parr, who rose and went into the dining room.

"Please have a seat, Mrs. Parr. This should take only a few minutes. And thank you for taking my telephone call earlier this morning. Did your greenskeeper speak to you before or after we were called?"

"Before", Mrs. Parr said. "As soon as William — our greenskeeper — told me what he had found, I asked him to call the police right away."

"Where are the others?" Mrs. Parr asked.

"Everyone who hasn't been interviewed is in the library. As I interview people, I'm asking each of you not to go into the library, and not to speak to anyone who hasn't been interviewed."

"Have you spoken to William, our greenskeeper?" Mrs. Parr asked.

"Yes", Campbell said curtly, while focusing on organizing herself for the interview.

"What time did you arrive at the club this morning, Mrs. Parr?"

"It was about seven o'clock."

"Isn't that rather early?"

"No. Not for me. I'm a vice president here. I had some administrative matters to deal with. And I'm meeting someone for lunch, so I wanted to get an early start on a leisurely round of golf this morning. Today will be a warm day, so I wanted to play while it's still reasonably cool."

"Who are you meeting?"

"The club treasurer, Molly Hendricks. We have a number of projects about to start and I want to make sure about their financing."

"Have you ever had trouble with prowlers, peeping Toms, anything like that?"

"Not that I'm aware of", Mrs. Parr replied.

"Does anyone know the details of your greenskeeper's discovery?"

"No", Mrs. Parr said without hesitation. "I'm pretty sure not, apart from the fact that a body has been discovered."

"So nobody knows that the body was found at the fourth hole?"

"No. But that statement is based on what I've heard in the clubhouse this morning, where nobody has mentioned anything about the fourth hole."

"Good. I'm going to insist that we keep it that way."

Mrs. Parr nodded her acknowledgement.

"Is there anything significant about the fourth hole?" Campbell asked.

"No. Not from a course design perspective. But we're contemplating some generic changes to aspects of the course, and we're testing some of them on the fourth hole." Mrs. Parr then described what that testing involved.

There were a few more questions about the club members, about functions held at the club, about how cash was handled. Mrs. Parr answered them all as best she could. The DC took what seemed to be comprehensive notes.

During the silent periods in this exchange, Mrs. Parr ranged over, in her mind, images of the club members, people who were friends, acquaintances, unknown quantities, and two or three that she secretly wished were not members at all. Two faces stood out. One, a Mrs. Grainger, was a lively and mentally attractive individual with whom Mrs. Parr had organized a lunch for the following week. The second was someone called Angela Poynting, one of the few members who was under thirty. She was pleasant, but cool, very self-possessed, and appeared to be interested in having only "golfing" relations with the other lady members. Perhaps this was because of the generally twenty-five plus years' age difference between her and the other ladies. But Mrs. Parr was also slightly puzzled by Mrs. Poynting's husband, who accompanied her to the club fairly regularly and was evidently devoted to her. Mrs. Poynting also entertained other consorts at the club, a variety of men of all ages who played rounds with her then joined her to sip drinks on the patio. Mrs. Poynting's husband was never present on those occasions. Nothing wrong with that, but for Mrs. Parr, the whole tenor of Mrs. Poynting's presence at and use of the club raised hordes of vague questions.

"May I ask you a few questions?" Mrs. Parr enquired of Campbell.

"Certainly. There might be very little I can say."

Mrs. Parr nodded and glanced briefly at her hands before raising her eyes and looking directly at the DC.

"Do you know who the man was?"

"Not yet."

"Do you know how long the body has been there?"

"No. But if I did know, I wouldn't be able to tell you."

"Do you know how he died?"

"Once again, I can't discuss that."

"Was it evident that any attempt had been made to hide the body?"

"I shouldn't be saying so, but no."

"So it was lying out in the open?"

"You could say that, yes."

"What do you mean, 'you could say that'?"

"Sorry. I can't discuss that. Just why are you asking these questions, Mrs. Parr."

"I'm curious", Mrs. Parr answered neutrally.

The DC looked through her notes, then began to rise, getting ready to dismiss Mrs. Parr.

"One more question, if I may", Mrs. Parr said.

The DC cocked her head.

"Did you find any shoe or boot impressions."

"I'm afraid I can't—"

"I take that to mean that there were no shoe impressions."

"I can't discuss that with you, Mrs. Parr. And I'm going to insist now that you tell me why you are asking these questions."

"I can. I have some responsibility for the running of this club. It is one of the oldest women's golf clubs in the world. It's a very good course, we are highly regarded, and we do everything we can to maintain our club's good image. So I want to satisfy myself that this crime, if that's what it is, will be investigated thoroughly and rigorously."

Campbell stiffened at this, but then forced herself to relax.

"And why would you have that concern?" There was a hint of steel behind her query.

"Because, DC Campbell, it's quite evident that you are not a golfer and that you know next to nothing about golf or golf courses. It might sound insulting, although I assure you that is not my intent, but my concern is that you could be looking directly at an important clue and not see it."

"Point taken, Mrs. Parr", Campbell said, somewhat more frostily now. "If I have any concerns I'll be sure to consult you", and she and Mrs. Parr exchanged business cards. "Please wait in the restaurant now."

It took about an hour and a half to interview the remaining ladies. The library slowly emptied, and in the restaurant, which filled slowly, there were faces that bore concerned, flustered, and apprehensive expressions. By ten forty-five, everyone had been interviewed and were told they could leave. Campbell stated, so that there would be no doubt, that the course most likely would be closed until about two o'clock that afternoon. The ladies all drifted silently back to the members' lounge, some to have another drink, but most just to collect their things and leave.

Just before noon, the medical examiner drove off in his car, along with a uniformed officer, who let the ME out past the police tape that barred the club entrance and waited there to let out the ambulance a little later. Immediately after that, the club's golf cart returned with William driving Campbell and two other uniformed police, who collected the officer stationed at the club entrance, took down the police tape, and left the property.

Mrs. Parr sought out William right away. They had a long chat, and William then went off, first to his small office in the maintenance sheds and then to speak to the head of security.

At one o'clock, Mrs. Parr met her lunch partner and they had a pleasant ninety-minute lunch and discussion. Mrs. Parr then went to the club office to catch up on some of the club's paperwork. William delivered the package she was expecting just before three that afternoon, and Mrs. Parr spent half an hour looking at the material and making notes. She then retired to a small room she called her "library" and spent about an hour thinking. She emerged wearing a determined, almost grim, expression, and decided that action was needed.

The telephone was answered after just two rings.

"DC Campbell here."

"Hello Detective Constable. This is Louise Parr at the Upper Canada Ladies' Golf Club."

"Hello Mrs. Parr. What can I do for you?" The tone was neutral but Mrs. Parr felt certain that her call was not welcome in the least.

"I wanted to ask how your investigation is proceeding."

There was a short silence from the other end, more ominous than pregnant.

"Mrs. Parr. It has been only a few hours, and this is not the only case I'm working on. I won't be discussing any aspect of this case with you, and I don't appreciate this interruption."

"I did tell you, Detective Constable, that I have a serious interest in making sure this situation is investigated thoroughly and quickly, and I'm simply following up on that concern."

From the other end of the line, the clipped and sharp response made clear the detective's impatience and rising anger.

"Mrs. Parr, I'm finding your meddling a nuisance. You are coming close to interfering with my efforts. I am going to hang up now. Please don't call me again—"

"I am certainly not trying to interfere, and if that's the impression I'm giving, then I do apologize. But I have information now indicating that the event you investigated this morning was a murder, and that I believe I might know who committed it."

Here there was a long silence.

"Mrs. Parr. I will warn you just this once. Interfering with a police investigation is a serious matter, and I won't hesitate to charge you if I think that's what you're doing. I want you to come to the precinct. It sounds as though you have information. We need to talk."

"I am not interfering. I have not interviewed anyone, I have not contaminated any scene, and I have not tampered with any evidence. And I resent you implying this. I will be at your office in half an hour and we can pick up the discussion there."

And she abruptly hung up.

Campbell had a tiny office, and although the piles of paper were neat and orderly, they were stacked high. Mrs. Parr entered and sat on the single guest chair. She noted that Campbell was now all business. She thought of the several hours of interviewing that had just been completed at the club, and realized that Campbell must have collected a good deal of information on the club and its members.

"I want to apologize straightaway, Detective Constable, if I gave the impression that I was being disrespectful in any way. I'm afraid that my commitment to our golf club sometimes can cloud my judgment."

"No offence taken, Mrs. Parr. But now let's get to the bottom of this — your claim to have found out something."

"Of course. I'll tell you exactly what I've done. After you left the club I spoke to William, the man who drove you and your officers out to the fourth hole. He gave me a full description of what he saw there. So I know that the body was found in a bunker, that it was lying on its back and was naked, and that that the corpse's hands were covering its genitals. I asked William to take a series of photographs of all the cars in the car park. I also asked him to have security download footage from all the security cameras from noon yesterday until the police left the club this afternoon."

"Why would you want pictures of the car park, Mrs. Parr?"

"To give us the chance of identifying non-members who might be on the grounds. We keep records of the licence numbers of all our members and staff, as well as those for contractors who come in to help maintain the course. Our club has several maintenance vehicles and one car, and the maintenance hut has a car-wash station so that we can keep these vehicles clean. A question of image. William is a very useful staff member, and we want to keep him, so we allow him to operate a private car-detailing service for members, up to two cars per day, very reasonable rates and he's allowed to keep the proceeds."

"And...?"

"And there were no cars parked whose licence numbers were not in our records, and no cars had remained there overnight. The course itself closes every evening at seven o'clock, but we don't have Fort Knox security to enforce that. We rely on members to finish their rounds promptly. The members' lounge remains open until about nine o'clock in the evening, unless there's some function—"

"Could you get right to the conclusions you've reached?"

Mrs. Parr laid out her reasons in a systematic explanation that took some time to work through, ending in a statement, almost a demand, that they should both return to the club. Campbell regarded her neutrally throughout, although Mrs. Parr could sense faint waves of disapproval emanating from the constable as she sat looking at the page and a half of notes she had made.

"What you have done concerns me, Mrs. Parr. If you haven't actually interfered with this investigation, you've certainly come awfully close." Her expression was hard.

Mrs. Parr's expression, which had remained open and transparent throughout her statement, now became one of impatience bordering on anger. She stood slowly and looked down at Campbell.

"Detective Constable, I can't help feeling that you are much more concerned about protecting the integrity, indeed the bloody sanctity, of your damned rules than you are about solving this case of murder at the fourth hole. Which is it?"

Campbell's expression was unfriendly. "It's both, Mrs. Parr. And I'm the one who will decide what sort of crime, if any, has been committed here. We're still investigating and—"

"Please, spare me, madam! We all know that it's a working hypothesis to be proved or disproved. So do me a favour, and let's not cavil and cavort on these logical pinheads. Time's a-wasting! You want to know the reasons for my concerns. For that, we need to return to the club. Shall we go?" And she turned and began walking determinedly from the room. Campbell had little option but to follow.

They took Campbell's car and the travel time to the golf club was about forty minutes. The first half of the trip was decidedly chilly, but then a few of those civilized pointless conversational remarks served to melt the metaphorical hoar frost from the car windows. Campbell asked many informal questions about the club and its members. There was a series of questions about any members who stood out, including those who played more regularly than most, those who used the club noticeably as a social venue, any members who set themselves apart from the other ladies for any reason. Mrs. Parr answered carefully.

"Our membership is quite varied, but almost all the ladies are retired professionals, all but a few are very sociable, and they are all avid and accomplished golfers."

"Do any of your members use the place just as a social club?"

"A few", Mrs. Parr replied. "There are four of our most senior members who come only for the three or four social events we have during the year. They still like the place, but all of them have conditions that make golf difficult."

"Anyone else?"

"There's me, and the other three members of the executive. We are here much more often than any other members, but we spend almost all that time on paperwork."

Mrs. Parr appeared to hesitate here, and Campbell's antennae detected this.

"Anyone else, Mrs. Parr?"

Mrs. Parr looked out the car window, hesitant, and appearing slightly ill at ease.

"Mrs. Parr?"

"There is one member, Angela Poynting. She is much younger than any of the other ladies, and she sponsors her husband…"

Campbell prodded Mrs. Parr once more.

"Mrs. Poynting also sponsors other gentlemen much more frequently than anyone else does."

"Is that unusual?"

"No. I wouldn't say unusual. Just different. Perhaps she just prefers playing golf with men."

"If she prefers playing golf with men, why not go to a regular golf course? Why come to a ladies course?"

"Maybe she does play elsewhere. I don't know."

"How is she regarded generally?"

"Well, she plays in ladies' foursomes."

"I'll ask again. How is she regarded? What do other ladies say about her?"

Mrs. Parr turned toward the driver's seat and looked steadily at DC Campbell.

"I'm uncomfortable talking about our members like this", she said evenly.

"And I'm sure you must also be uncomfortable, Mrs. Parr, at having a body discovered on your course, and that you would be far more uncomfortable at the possibility that you might not do as much as you could to help us explain that."

Mrs. Parr nodded and looked away.

"You're right, of course." After a short delay, she continued. "Mrs. Poynting is considered to be socially distant."

"Do people dislike her?"

"Some probably do. That's to be expected in any group of people. But I'm not aware of any active dislike."

By the time they arrived at the club car park, they shared a more common view of the situation.

As they pulled up in front of the clubhouse, Mrs. Parr noticed that, even though it was now late in the day, Mrs. Poynting's car was in the members' car park, and she noted that fact to Campbell. She expected that it would take some time to locate Mrs. Poynting, but as luck would have it, they met her in the largish circulation area. She had just emerged from the bar and was headed with her drink toward the patio.

"May we join you?" Mrs. Parr asked.

Mrs. Poynting inclined her head slightly, without a smile.

They found a small table in one of the distant corners of the patio next to an immaculately sculpted privet hedge. The sun was now heading for the western horizon but beamed late afternoon heat from a sparse cumulus sky. Birds sang with real gusto, exultant chirps that could easily be mistaken for hole-in-one exclamations. A muffled grass mower hummed contentedly in the distance. Mrs. Parr recognized in all this the many reasons why she loved the club so much and the root of her determination to see that it was run properly.

Campbell pulled out her notebook and pen, and Mrs. Parr smiled reassuringly.

"I'm sorry to intrude on your day Mrs. Poynting, but I have just a few questions for you."

"Is this about that dreadful occurrence on—"

Campbell cut off this interjection by deliberately not looking at Mrs. Poynting then making a rather dramatic show of leafing through her notebook. She stopped to study briefly a few earlier annotations, then found a blank page. She looked up at Mrs. Poynting and smiled. The smile was not returned.

"Your husband plays here sometimes. Is that correct?"

"My husband? Well, yes. But what's that got to do with—"

"When did he play here last?" Campbell interrupted, in a manner perhaps best described as insensitive plod.

Calmly, Mrs. Poynting turned toward Mrs. Parr. "And just why are you involved in this — inquisition?"

Mrs. Parr opened her mouth to reply, but was cut off by Campbell.

"At my request. The question, please, Mrs. Poynting."

Still calm, Mrs. Poynting turned her head slowly to direct a very icy stare at Campbell.

"It was the day before yesterday."

"And you were here with him?" Campbell asked.

"Of course. He can't attend unless a member signs him in."

"And that was the day before, no, two days before the body was found?"

"If you say so", Mrs. Poynting replied, not trying to hide her impatience and contempt. "You're the investigator."

"And did you play that day?"

"No. Gerald played with three others."

"And are you playing today?" Campbell asked pleasantly, almost as though she expected to be asked to join in.

"'Hoping' is the word", was Mrs. Poynting's withering reply, "although it looks like even a late round might have to be missed just to answer a lot of useless questions."

Campbell made a note, then looked up and smiled as though she had just been handed the key that would unlock the mystery.

"Does your husband keep any gear in your locker here at the club? His irons? Golfing caps? His shoes, perhaps?"

"Yes. But I don't see—"

"I'd like to see your locker now, please", Campbell said, putting away her pen and notebook and beginning to rise, a signal that they were going to the locker right away and that further discussion was out of the question.

They all rose and made their way through the club, which was more crowded than usual for this late in the day.

"This is my locker", Mrs. Poynting said coldly.

Campbell made an impatient sign, and Mrs. Poynting spun the combination lock, opened the locker, and stood back. Campbell used her pen to lift and to pull aside various items in the locker.

"Are those your husband's golfing shoes?" she asked, pointing to a pair of largish shoes at the bottom of the locker, neatly set next to a pair of much smaller shoes.

"Yes." Same very brusque manner.

Campbell pulled out a large clear plastic evidence bag and a black felt-tipped pen. "I'm going to have to take his shoes. I'll give you a receipt for them."

Mrs. Poynting's lips now formed a bloodless white slash.

"What? Just what is going on here Madame Vice-President?" she asked, turning a laser glare toward Mrs. Parr.

"It's a simple matter. Eliminating people from the inquiry", Campbell intoned, and she pulled on a blue latex glove, picked up the shoes, placed them in the bag, sealed it, and made a felt-tipped annotation on the bag.

"Eliminating people? Shoes? This is ridiculous! How can shoes—"

"The sand", Campbell said enigmatically. "Sand on the shoes will tell us whether he's been in a bunker lately."

"Hah!" Mrs. Poynting laughed mirthlessly. "Gerald is not a great golfer. He seems to spend most of his day in bunkers. Even the best golfers have to get out of bunkers occasionally. And anyway. Sand is sand!"

"As I understand things, that's not true", Campbell stated. "Bunker sand is treated. So not all sand is just sand."

"Do you have any idea", Mrs. Poynting began in withering contempt, "how many bunkers there are on this course?"

"What you might not be aware of Angela", Mrs. Parr interjected calmly, "is that our maintenance company is testing a new chemical treatment for bunker sand. And only a few of the bunkers are guinea-pigs for that testing."

Mrs. Poynting waved that off impatiently. "Are we through here?" she asked icily.

"Yes", Campbell replied in a chipper tone, stowing her notebook and rising. "Thank you, Mrs. Poynting." Campbell nodded to Mrs. Parr and headed for the exit and the guest car park. Mrs. Parr said nothing to Mrs. Poynting and headed toward the club's executive offices.

About half an hour later, in response to a call from Mrs. Parr, there was a knock on the door to the executive offices. Mrs. Parr greeted her guest and they left together for the members' changing area. Mrs. Poynting was there and had just removed a pair of golf shoes from her locker and transferred them to a sports bag.

"If you're off to play some golf, won't you need those shoes, Mrs. Poynting?"

Mrs. Poynting turned abruptly and looked in surprise at Detective Constable Campbell and Mrs. Parr.

"No. No … I-I'm not going to play golf. I've just decided that I need some new golf shoes."

"May I see them?" Campbell asked calmly.

"They're just golf shoes", Mrs. Poynting replied, now having recovered her suave and aloof manner. "What possible interest could they be to you?"

"May I see them?" Campbell repeated. Mrs. Poynting handed over the carrier bag she was holding with evident reluctance. Campbell took the bag, opened it, and peered in.

"They look like perfectly good shoes to me. What do you think, Mrs. Parr?"

Mrs. Parr neither looked at the shoes nor replied.

"I will need to take these shoes, Mrs. Poynting", Campbell said, unfolding another evidence bag, and sliding shoes and carrier bag into it.

"This is ridiculous!" Mrs. Poynting objected loudly, bristling from anger. "Are you going to put up with this harassment, Mrs. Parr?"

Mrs. Parr looked at Mrs. Poynting in rising impatience. "This is a police investigation, Mrs. Poynting, and it's well out of my hands. But I do suggest that if we are going to discuss these matters, we do it in private in the club's executive offices." And she then led the other two to the office where she spent so much time on the club's operation, activities, and investments.

Behind closed doors, Mrs. Poynting was much more vocal and demanding.

"This is outrageous!" she said angrily to Campbell. "I'll be talking to your superiors. I want my property back *right now*. You have no—"

"Sit down Mrs. Poynting", Campbell ordered, a hard edge in her voice.

"I will not sit down. I'm calling my lawyer." She pulled a cellphone from her handbag.

"Your privilege, Mrs. Poynting. But you are not in custody or under arrest. In fact, you are free to go, if that's what you wish."

"That's exactly what I plan to do", and she held out her hand. "My shoes, please."

"No", Campbell said firmly. "The shoes stay with me. I will be taking them straight to the forensics lab for testing."

At that point Campbell regarded Mrs. Poynting, then opened the bag and glanced again at the shoes.

"These shoes look large for you Mrs. Poynting. What's your shoe size?"

"I can't believe this! My shoe size?"

"Let me have your opinion Mrs. Parr", Campbell said, holding open the bag. Mrs. Parr gazed in at the shoes.

She shook her head. "No idea really."

"Would you mind trying on one of these shoes, Mrs. Poynting?" Campbell asked.

"Yes I would mind. I would mind very much."

Campbell drew out her cellphone, tapped it a few times, and laid it on the table facing Mrs. Poynting.

"Do you know this person Mrs. Poynting?" The picture on the cellphone was the face of the dead man.

Mrs. Poynting glanced at the phone. "No. No idea", she said, looking away quickly.

"You don't know him? Never seen him before?"

Turning to Mrs. Parr, Campbell asked "Have you seen this man before Mrs. Parr?" Mrs. Parr hesitated briefly.

"I don't know who he is, but I've seen him in the restaurant here."

"Often?"

"No. I wouldn't say often. But several times."

"Have you seen him with Mrs. Poynting?"

Mrs. Parr thought for a moment. "I don't think so, but I can't say with certainty."

"That's okay", Campbell said. "We can ask other members."

They both looked at Mrs. Poynting. She ignored them and began speaking into her cellphone, evidently talking to a lawyer. She finished the call, put the cellphone down, and glared at the other two women.

"My lawyer will be here in half an hour. I'm not answering any more questions until he arrives."

"That's fine Mrs. Poynting. I'll point out, however, that you're free to go at any time."

"Not without my shoes."

"Not happening", Campbell said bluntly. She looked once more at Mrs. Poynting.

"You can be sure, Mrs. Poynting, that we will be uncovering all the facts in this case. Who was where and when. Attendance by members and guests at this club going back as far as necessary. The forensic evidence concerning these shoes. All the details of the person whose body was found at the sixth hole. Every piece of—"

"Sixth ho—?"

Too late, Mrs. Poynting saw the trap.

From that point, it surprised both Campbell and Mrs. Parr how quickly Mrs. Poynting just gave up. Her tone became deflated and defeated, and Campbell took several pages of notes, before taking her cellphone from her pocket and entering a number.

"Please come in now, Constable Tracey. We're in the executive offices."

A few minutes later, a youngish constable knocked on the door and entered. Campbell gave the constable his instructions, informed Mrs. Poynting that she was under arrest and read her her rights, then nodded to the constable who took Mrs. Poynting by the elbow and began to lead her toward the door.

"Detective Constable", Mrs. Parr began. "Would you consider having your constable take Mrs. Poynting out this way?" and she indicated another door behind her. "Through the kitchens and out the back?"

Campbell nodded her agreement to the constable.

"Out this door, Constable", Mrs. Parr instructed, and then she gave directions on how to reach the car park unobserved.

"Thank you", Mrs. Poynting said, directing a wan smile toward Mrs. Parr.

Mrs. Parr directed at her a hard uncomplimentary look.

"Please don't think I'm doing this for you, Angela. My only concern is the good name of this club." Saying that, she turned her back on Mrs. Poynting.

After Mrs. Poynting and the constable had left, Campbell looked at Mrs. Parr, smiled briefly, then thanked her for her help.

"Just a few further points to clear up", Campbell began. "What was it that raised your suspicions about Mrs. Poynting?"

Mrs. Parr thought for a few moments. "I have to admit, Detective Constable, somewhat to my shame, that I never really had a good feeling about Angela. She came here as a very young woman, at least compared to the rest of us, but then she seemed to make no effort to mix. Her first husband died young, apparently from congenital heart problems, and left her holding a twenty-million-dollar estate. The day after his funeral, she was here playing golf. She then married her current husband, Gerald Poynting, who is almost thirty-five years her senior. Okay. The heart has its ways and the head knows them not. All this might sound like gossip … but even though Angela played here with Gerald, she sponsored other men far more frequently. A name that I saw regularly in our guest book was Ramon Abrego. Never met him. Don't know what he looks like. Don't even know whether it's a portmanteau name that provides entry to several different men."

"Have you asked?" Campbell inquired.

"And what would I ask? 'Excuse me, Angela. How many men named Ramon Abrego do you know?' That's not what we do here."

"What made you suspect there was some connection between this death and Gerald?"

"Two things", Mrs. Parr began after a few moments thought, evidently taking time to marshal her points. "First, there has been more than one instance that indicated Gerald is possessive, given to fits of jealousy."

"Anything serious?" Campbell asked.

"Nothing like a fight or a violent outburst. But Gerald is quite a transparent individual. It was evident on many occasions that he was not happy at the attention Angela was paying to other men, especially younger men."

"Anything else?" Campbell prodded.

"Yes. Just how do I put this … William told me later that the body was that of a rather handsome young man, dark wavy hair … and that although he had rather large hands they still weren't large enough to cover all his, er, endowment."

Campbell maintained a neutral expression.

"I know, I know", Mrs. Parr hurried to add. "Comments like that about a man can be every bit as offensive as comments about the size of a woman's breasts. The point here is that this is something that William had no need to tell me, except these are things that can matter a great deal to some men."

"And you suspect that Gerald might be one of those men?"

"I have no idea", Mrs. Parr said with emphasis. "But it's possible."

"And?"

"And nothing", Mrs. Parr countered. "But if the man out there in the bunker had been one of Angela's boys, well, Gerald might have had a reason to step in. Everyone has their limit."

The two women looked at one another and nodded.

"But instead", Campbell began.

"Yes, instead your intuition, Detective Constable, was bang on the mark. It was Mrs. Poynting who did the dirty deed. She left no doubt that she felt that the cad was after her money. That she was being subject to extortion. That her good name was at risk. She's admitted it to us both, and the sand on her golf shoes likely will be the smoking gun. Not that one is needed now."

Campbell began gathering papers and file folders, preparing to depart.

"I think that's it, Mrs. Parr. Thank you for your time. I've learned something today."

Campbell rose to leave, shook Mrs. Parr's hand, the two smiled at each other, and Campbell moved toward the door. But then she stopped and turned back.

"Is there any chance that … sometime … perhaps…" Campbell's question faded.

Mrs. Parr's face broke into a bright and friendly smile.

"Yes, of course. And let's agree to call each other Louise and Helen. Please drop in any time, giving me a bit of advance notice, of course. I'd be delighted to give you your introduction to our wonderful sport."

Walking With Albert

It was just before dusk. A hole had been punched somewhere in the western side of the great celestial sphere, and the last of the day's light was draining away slowly through it. The sky softened through a range of colours, and the red volcanic rock that formed the city wall slowly lost its warm glow, cooled, and darkened. I reminded myself that I was here, in Ulm, on something of a technical pilgrimage.

The masticatory crunch of gravel on the path and the river that burbled and whispered to my right were my only companions. Turning through an opening in the Ulm city wall, I began walking along Fischergasse, which rose before me, leading to the centre. An earlier light shower had coated the cobbles and rendered them luminous in the failing light of day.

The *Fischerviertel* was all around me, a delightful jumble of centuries-old houses, some of them faithfully rebuilt to repair bomb damage. Water from the small River Blau splashed around and between the houses, making the whole scene a multi-media display of caprice and unpredictability. *Das schiefe Haus*, the most lop-sided building in the world, chuckled as it flaunted its unending open challenge to gravity. Having seen only pictures of it, I looked at it for a moment, a fifteenth century half-timbered German house, steeply pitched roof, but twisted and leaning at what seemed an impossible angle.

It was just about then I realized he was walking next to me.

We walked over the cobbles together, our steps almost in unison, the volumes of air around us filled by the white noise from the water. Somehow, his presence seemed natural and normal. I remember being neither surprised, nor overwhelmed, nor intimidated. It felt as though he were a friend. I looked across at him and he smiled. His eyes managed, at the same time, to appear sad, knowing, and mischievous. He ran a hand absent-mindedly though his shock of white hair, an action that did nothing to tame its unruliness.

We spoke about the city. He talked in a quiet voice about how it had changed, while in many ways remaining the same. His gaze followed the irregular lines of the buildings, and his attraction to the streets, the houses, the pervading spirit of the city, as it had been back then, shone through.

We climbed a street that opened into the *Marktplatz* surrounding the *Rathaus*. He looked up at the solid façade of the *Rathaus* and nodded. We crossed the *Marktplatz* and headed toward the massive form of the Minster, which loomed benevolently ahead of us. The soaring upper reaches of the vast building caught the light that still swarmed high in the air and beamed it down toward us in a smile of benediction. As we passed along the flank of the enormous structure, he looked up, scanning the elaborate stonework and graceful windows that expressed skyward yearning.

He then spoke of his early life, his unsettled and indifferent schooling, his voice carrying notes of regret, mild astonishment, acceptance, and humour. It took several minutes to stroll out in front of the Minster, and by this time, the spire, the tallest church spire in the world, was catching the last light of the day, and it attracted our gaze as a beacon. We both stopped and craned our necks. It was a sublime moment.

He broke his silence once more, this time speaking of his life, work, and achievements, and a flicker of pride shimmered across his face. His voice was low and light, and while it carried hints of what might have been, what this city might have meant to him, it reflected also the many dark portents that all too soon had become a grim and unspeakable Nazi reality. From his gaze, as he continued to scan the simple complexity of the spire, I could see overwhelming nostalgia, deep regret, but a stark conviction that his personal past had unfolded in the only way possible, that there was nothing more he could have done for those who became trapped in the inferno. I was dying to ask him many questions, but felt somehow that I couldn't, that I shouldn't, that this chance to enjoy his presence should be taken just for what it was, a unique gift.

The last of the day's light moved higher into the sky, clinging to the spire until finally, quietly, it slipped free, and the entire Minster slid gently into shadow. He continued gazing upward for a few minutes, then turned to face me. He smiled once more, and his hair formed a fuzzy silhouette against the noctilucent western sky. He offered me his hand and we shook.

"I have enjoyed your company", he said simply, the smile still animating his face and carrying soft lights into his eyes. A dozen thoughts clambered within me for expression, but the vocal machinery had frozen.

Ask him something! Tell him something! Say something! came the imperious internal commands, but all I could do was smile. His return smile broadened as he nodded again, appearing to understand my quandary, my distress, my fear that a great opportunity was slipping from my grasp.

"Where will you go now?" I managed to sputter in a half-croak, absurdly, irrelevantly, and not having the slightest idea how I had chosen such a mundane, prosaic utterance.

"I'm going home. To my home here in Ulm. Where I was born. It doesn't mean a lot to me now, but there are things I want to see again."

No!

He can't leave now!

Not like this!

"It's near the railway station, my home. It's been some time since I saw it last." He looked around again somewhat uncertainly, and there was once more that sense of longing, but at the same time an acceptance of destiny, of the finality of events. A last flicker of a smile, he began turning to leave, and then I blurted out:

"But do you have any advice, anything to say to me?"

His body was half-turned as he stopped and his head came round in order to look into my face. The quiet and unassuming power of his presence was overwhelming.

"We live in different worlds, young man. Mine is all but gone. I wouldn't dare make suggestions about your world or how you should approach it." — he seemed to sense my my desire for him to say something more…

"I was granted some insights into space and time, and for those I have been and remain most humbly grateful. You need to explore your world, my young friend, but you should accept, and not lose, what others before you have learned."

Here, he hesitated.

"I suspect that in finding the insight and the strength to challenge assumptions, you will also find your way."

I thought immediately of Planck and Heisenberg.

Those sad, knowing eyes fixed mine for a few seconds longer. A smile tugged once more at the corners of his mouth, then he turned and began walking back the way we had come, along the Minster, toward the *Marktplatz*, and from there he would then turn down toward the railway station. The air was chilling rapidly, and ragged sheets of mist were drifting into the city from the river.

He had moved about ten metres away from me.

A lone swirl of mist engulfed him. When it cleared, only a second later, he was no longer there.

A feeling of unreality pervaded the place, since I knew that his family home near the railway station had disappeared long since. But his words were armour against any sense of illusion.

I had no doubt.

I had met Albert Einstein.

Le Chat Moïse

Oddly enough, the cat was the first thing we saw.

"Oh! Comme il est beau, ce chat! Comment s'appelle-t-il?

"Il s'appelle Moïse." *Moses*, I thought. *Now how would a cat come by a name like that?*

Moïse lay sprawled on a long table, and despite the attention being paid to him, or perhaps even because of it, he didn't raise an eyebrow. His entire demeanour radiated boredom, as though he were saying "Dear God! When will these frightful people leave? Could somebody please bring me another decent bottle of Châteauneuf-du-Pape?"

It was the perfect setting. Late afternoon in mid-September. The drive along the extended and elegant avenue, leading to the main building at Château Mousset, had certainly spiked our interest. All four of us, me and my wife, Liz, and our friends Marie and Richard, were old hands at wine tours. Once inside, we found that we had the place to ourselves. The day was warm, but it was that comfortable early autumn warmth of the Avignon region. We had taken a long route from the parking lot to the tasting area, strolling past the ends of the rows of vines, and could feel the day's heat, now being radiated back at us, having been stored in the fist-sized stones covering the ground in the scrupulously maintained vineyards. Inside the tasting room, it was cool and delicious. The richly layered aromas of moulds and yeasts, long-acclimatized to this place they now called home, mingled sensuously with the fruity sharpness of freshly pressed grape juice. In the light of those recognized scents, I glanced over at Moïse once again. I couldn't tell whether he was being a naturally languid cat, or if he had spent so much time in here, he was permanently hammered.

Sylvain, the man behind the tasting bar, didn't need to practise his English. I knew he was Sylvain from the discreet little nametag pinned to his shirt.

"Allow me to compliment you on your French, sir", Sylvain said in modestly accented English. His voice was as smooth and rich as I imagined the best vintage Château Mousset would be.

"Are you here to do some tasting mesdames, messieurs?"

"Ah, non!" I said. "Nous sommes venus ici pour faire la connaissance de votre chat."

I was pleased to see Sylvain stumble, then recover when he got the joke — two people coming all that way just to get to know his cat! The delay here was long enough for me to construct the next riposte, in the event I should need one. From that point, we continued in French, everyone smiling sweetly and making all those deferring gestures universally interpreted to mean that honour would be served. Translating from that point, our conversation continued as follows.

"Yes", my wife said, admiring the bottles ranged behind the tasting bar. "We would love to try your wines. I adore your Château des Fines Roches and Domaine des Quatre Vents", all without even a glance at the tasting menu.

"Indeed", I continued, "and I am an absolute fan of rosés, even though where I come from, people scoff at me for offering rosé with steak."

Sylvain was good. He didn't bat an eyelid. And he was just about to regain control of the conversation and the tasting, when Richard broke in suavely.

"But there's time for all this, I'm sure. We're in no particular rush, and these things should all be pursued without undue haste. Please tell us a bit more about Moïse. It's not often one sees a cat in a tasting room, and especially not one as relaxed and sophisticated as he is."

"Well, there's not that much to tell. What can I say? Moïse is a cat."

"Yes, evidently", Marie replied, "but that's an extraordinary table he's lying on. I'm sure that table reminds me of something. A writer, perhaps?"

Sylvain's face showed suddenly increased focus. Marie had his attention.

"Madame has a truly acute eye. The table is indeed significant. Please, take a closer look at it."

We all moved toward the table. Moïse opened one eye, trying to decide whether our massed approach signalled food or disturbance.

Richard found it first — a small metal plate about one centimetre by four, tacked to the edge of the table top at one of the long ends. On the plate was the word "FONTVIEILLE".

"Fontvieille must mean Daudet. Did this come from his windmill?" my wife asked.

"Indeed it did, as far as I can tell", Sylvain replied, now completely comfortable speaking to us. "It was likely on this table that he wrote his 'Lettres'."

Marie scratched Moïse's head, and he relaxed even more, realizing that while disturbance could be dismissed as a concern, he had missed an alternative that was better even than food: attention.

"And how about Moïse?" I asked. "How did he acquire that name?"

"Well, he came by it honestly", Sylvain said past a slow smile. "He's a foundling, of course. I was training vines one day and had stopped for lunch. I was at that picnic table just out there", and he pointed to a burgundy table visible through the window next to the bar.

"There were eight of them. Moïse was evidently the alpha male. Couldn't have been more than about four weeks old. Moïse just led the other seven out of the vineyard and walked them right up to my table."

We all looked again at Moïse, this leader of his own feline exodus. The cat stretched again, squinted at us, then yawned luxuriously, as if to say that it was no big deal, and that the incentive behind it all should be evident from his current "promised land".

I looked over at Richard and knew that he was thinking about Daudet's unsavoury views, expressed late in his life, on Dreyfus in particular and on Jews in general.

Sylvain was tall, about thirty-five, had the swarthy complexion and dark curly hair often associated with Provence. But I took him for a town dweller. Perhaps he lived nearby in Avignon or Orange, or maybe even in Saint-Rémy-de-Provence.

It might have been the curious, inquiring way my wife looked at Sylvain.

"It was me who took in Moïse", Sylvain explained. "And I found homes for the other seven kittens. They were all black as well, just like

Moïse. And although I work here, I'm also an investor, part-owner, and I live in a small cottage just down the road at Sorgues."

"Did you find the table?" Marie asked.

"Yes."

"Is it really Daudet's writing table?"

"Possibly. But I don't really care. The label was fastened to it when I bought it at an antique dealer's sale. For me, it's the idea that's important."

We did some wine tasting. It was all very good, of course, and Sylvain, now entirely comfortable speaking to us in French, even drifting occasionally into local expressions, told us about the wines, the vineyards, the *terroir*. And we spent a very leisurely and informative hour there.

We bought several bottles, said an extended farewell to Sylvain, and walked out into the warm, still air of late afternoon.

I had already decided that first thing the next morning I would find a bookshop and pick up a copy of *Lettres de mon moulin*. I had studied it in high school and had read it again a couple of decades later, but didn't have my own copy.

My strong recollection, the image that came back to me from Daudet's letters, was of a time and place that was peaceful, full of characters, and utterly rural — almost an imaginary place, a place we would all like to visit. This recollection was accompanied closely by a clear memory of statements made by one of my professors on what he called a 'tricky area of literature', to be careful about knowing when to let knowledge of an author's life and views influence, or not influence, how one judges his work.

It fit also the slow pace of our visit to Château Mousset, having the large tasting room all to ourselves, enjoying the sensual immersion in September sunlight, aromas that were the place's unique signature of wine, the colours reaching out from our tasting glasses, Sylvain's explanations, and Daudet's table linking us to another world. It was one of those magical hours.

And then there was Moïse.

The cat who made it all so memorable.

"Le Chat Moïse" is based on a real experience of the author, his wife, and two friends.

Just Rocks

It was too early in the day for the streets of Rosseau to be clogged by the usual July tourist traffic. During the summer months, and anywhere near the three big lakes in Muskoka, one had to plan one's time carefully. We had done that, Jim and I.

Our wives had gone off to the Shaw Festival. When a theatre outing had been proposed, months earlier, I had thought that it would be fun. At the time, there had been no discussion of specifics, but that was fine. I was content just to wait.

After quite a few weeks had gone by, I raised the matter obliquely, and picked up the message that it was going to be a girls' weekend. That was okay too. Not a snub; our foursome ventures were frequent and varied, but so were our twosome outings.

That was how Jim and I came to be spending a long weekend in Muskoka. It was partly for the scenery, but mainly just another occasion for us to discuss physics. That sounds bizarre to most people when they hear of it, but Jim and I are both passionate about our subject, and we have shared that keen interest since we first met in our late teens. Our lives unfolded in what one might call a prosaic way, me finding an early niche in consulting to industry and Jim making a professional home in academia, straight from his doctorate.

We left at half past five on Friday morning. Traffic was light; we sped out of town and were cruising past Barrie well before seven. The day was bright and fresh, we were already deep into physics discussions, and by nine o'clock, we were just where we had planned to be: seated at the Cottage Law Canteen waiting for our blowout breakfasts to be delivered. After breakfast, we would check into the historic B&B, then set out on our planned activities for the weekend, all of which were just backdrops for more discussions.

"Bon appétit, messieurs!"

"Merci bien!" we chimed in unison, then smirked happily at one another.

We began working on our meals. The food really was delicious.

"You're not going to be farting all day, are you?"

"Well, I hope so", I replied brightly. "But I'm not sure what brought out that question. The broccoli, perchance?"

"The broccoli indeed. Broccoli for breakfast?"

"Ever heard of Coxeter?" I ventured. "The geometer", I added a few seconds later in response to dead air time and blank gaze.

"Yes. But what's that got—"

"He lived to the age of ninety-six", I said reverently.

"And?"

"Well, and then he died."

"It's a bit early for you to be suffering from sunstroke, isn't it?"

"The point is that broccoli was just about all he ate. Raw broccoli and olive oil."

"I knew there was a reason I hated geometry. So, you've ordered a side dish of broccoli for breakfast because your geometric skills are failing. Some kind of Popeye remedy, is that it?"

This conversational descent into a pointless leguminous byway was terminated as we seriously dug into the two large plates of very appealing food.

"So. Here we are", I said. I had finished my back bacon and turned to the eggs and home fries.

"Yes", Jim agreed through a smile, as he sequestered a piece of his own bacon that he felt, evidently, was about to defect to my plate. "What shall we do today?"

"I think we do proper justice to this meal, have a decent amount of coffee, check into the B&B, then go for a walk in the morning and you can tell me how your work on sonoluminescence has been going."

"Certainly. But you'll need to bring me up to date on your work as well."

"Boring by comparison", I said, taking a sip of coffee. "It's just an endless series of tasks to make sure that heat is transferred, or not transferred, and to provide means for making perfect measurements in both those situations. Oh! And always the warnings to stay within hard parsimonious limits on time and dollar budgets."

"Nice display of outraged heat, but I don't believe a word of it. You consultants are rolling in it. Besides, I saw your last paper. Brilliant. You should publish more."

"I don't need to face the academic firing squad", I countered. "Not like you. In any case, I need to wait another few months."

"Why?"

"The only time I can be academically creative is in winter, when my garret is cold and draughty, and the food runs low."

A companionable silence gathered around us as we finished our meals. More coffee came our way, we finished it at leisure, and then turned our chairs to face the sun. The heat of the day was rising, but the air was fresh.

"After we check in, how about a walk by the lake?" I asked.

"With pleasure! Lead on, sir!"

We set off, dropped our bags at the B&B, then headed for the church and Water Street. The village was becoming busy, in its typical random-walk tourist fashion. Rosseau Bay opened out onto the panorama of Lake Rosseau. Stunning. We strolled along, hoping to give the appearance of two guys oblivious to everyday realities, in the grip of profound thoughts.

Without any prodding, Jim began describing some of his latest research. He warmed to the subject quickly, and it was apparent that he was just as pleased to have made recent progress as he was to be working on tough problems. We walked on, came to a boat rental place, and arranged a canoe for an hour. We weren't going anywhere in particular. The discussion flowed freely, the water lapped canoe sides and paddles, and dramatic shoulders of igneous rock heaved out of the lake, looking like giant telluric monsters off for their morning dip. Our discussion continued, ranging briefly over non-technical topics, but always returning to the welcoming turf of physics and mathematics.

As we handed the canoe back to the rental guy, Jim suggested an ice cream, a stand being conveniently close. We carried our cones to a nearby bench. At some point in our discussions, the topic of fashionable physics, *prima donna* physics, always arose, as it did now, prompting yet again our mock amazement at how the organizational headaches and budgetary strains still failed to dampen people's ardour for Big Physics. Our own shared personal delight in and commitment to physics flowed from those exquisite little pockets of unexplained effects that lurk everywhere, are there for the asking, and seldom require more than a notepad and pencil, a computer or calculator, and occasionally a few good reference books. Looking out across the lake, we could scan numerous great jagged blocks of stone rising dramatically from the water. It was rugged, fantastic, overwhelming.

Jim had pulled out the retractable pointer that, inexplicably, he always carried, and was drawing doodles in the gravel path in front of our bench.

"Did you ever track down that quote?" he asked.

"The one from Uhlenbeck? 'The frontiers of physics are all around us'"?

"That's the one. Great quote! Where did he write it?"

"He didn't."

"It's not an Uhlenbeck quote?" he asked in surprise.

"Oh, it is. But it's a statement he made, not something he wrote. I got that from a guy at UCLA. One of Uhlenbeck's PhD students."

"Really? You spoke to him?"

"No, but just as good. Email. It was a statement Uhlenbeck made at some point. It impressed the student, and he jotted it down."

"That's a lot better than something written … almost like it's just ours!"

"Well, it is. At least it is at second hand."

Jim smiled suddenly, as though he had just come up with some new killer angle on wave function collapse. His doodling in the gravel became more vigorous, more determined. It looked like he was tinkering with something in spherical co-ordinates. But after a minute or so, the doodling tapered off, and Jim began glancing around distractedly.

I looked across at him. "Don't worry, Archimedes. There aren't any Roman soldiers about."

Jim continued looking around, then turned and looked behind us. About five feet away, a boy about ten years old was watching us.

"Hi", Jim said. "I'm Jim; this is Chris. What's your name?"

"What are you drawing?" the boy asked.

"Well, I'm not really drawing anything. I'm fiddling with formulas. Do you live here?"

"No", the boy said, now a bit more hesitant. "My mom and dad are just over there", and he pointed to a couple relaxing on a bench about thirty feet away. "We're here for a week."

"Give me one of your business cards, Jim", I said. He did and I got up and left. I returned, accompanied by the boy's mother. She eyed us closely. I said to the boy, but also glancing at his mother for her agreement, "Come around and sit with us." The boy looked at his mother.

"It's okay Michael", and she waved him to take a seat on our bench. We moved well apart and Michael sat between us.

"Is that like arithmetic?" Michael asked, pointing to Jim's scratchings in the sand. "A bit", Jim said. "Do you like arithmetic?"

"Yes", the boy said, now more enthusiastic and less cautious. "But that doesn't look like arithmetic."

"Well, no", Jim said. "It's a bit more complicated than that." Michael's mother had now moved a few feet further away. She was smiling.

"Are you a teacher?" Michael asked. "Do you teach arithmetic?" We talked more, Jim and me taking turns. Michael opened up more, and became frankly curious when we told him what we do for a living.

"Physics?" he said, as an open-ended expression of youthful curiosity and puzzlement.

Jim talked, taking the lead, since he's a natural teacher. "So, we study basically anything, and everything."

"Everything?" Michael said.

"Yes, everything. The sky — and I can tell you why it's blue — the clouds — and I can tell you what they are and why they look the way they do — this water — and I can tell you all sorts of things about water — and those rocks."

"They're just rocks", Michael said.

"Well", Jim began, "they're more than just rocks. Those are some of the oldest rocks in the world. And a long time ago, they weren't rocks, they were red-hot liquid, and they're made of stuff that came from a long, long way away."

"Stuff? What kind of stuff?"

"Stuff called elements. In those rocks there's silicon, oxygen, aluminum, potassium, sodium, calcium, iron, titanium, and lots more. There's only one place those things can come from."

The boy looked from one to the other of us. Jim had him hooked. "Where?"

"From inside one of those", Jim said, pointing at the sun.

Now the boy was really interested. "The sun?"

"Well, not that sun, not *our* sun, but one something like it."

"How did all that stuff get from there to here?"

"It happened a very long time ago, but back then, that other sun was bigger than our sun, quite a bit bigger, it burned brightly but not for very long, and then it blew up and threw all those elements out into space. When our solar system formed, some of that stuff became our Earth, and eventually some of it became those rocks. So, you see, it's hardly fair to say that they're 'just rocks'. They have a fantastic story to tell."

The boy looked at the rocks. He looked at each of us. Then he sat silently for quite a long time. He climbed off the bench and stood before us.

"Thanks, er, mister." He began to move away. After only two steps, he turned back toward us.

"Where could I, um…"

I smiled at him, looked over at Jim, then looked back at Michael.

"I'll send you something to read about all this, Michael", I said.

He nodded distractedly.

"Thanks. Thanks…", he said, then hurried off to his parents.

"How are you going to send him anything?" Jim asked.

"I got his father's business card."

We sat and watched Michael walk back to where his parents were. He was talking to them, then he pointed at the sun. Jim and I waved at them, they smiled and waved back.

Warm smiles. Understanding smiles. Grateful smiles, I thought.

We watched the three of them get up and walk back along the bay.

"I think we've done a decent day's work", I said.

"Indeed", Jim replied. "Another young mind off on its road to Damascus."

For a few minutes we shared the energy sent to us from the sun, and another warm feeling that came from somewhere else altogether.

"About that talk you gave last month on bubble dynamics", I said, once again in critical scientific mode. "I think you got part of it wrong."

"Oh? And what would you know about…"

Anything Goes

The occasion called for a poke in the eye.

"*Wer hat Dich die Erlaubnis gegeben hier zu sitzen?*" (Who gave you permission to sit here?)

I waited for a response. Coming out of the blue, the question and its insulting tone was enough to spoil anyone's moment. But that didn't happen.

I was impressed. After only about a two-second delay he was ready with a reply.

"Just when I thought I was having a perfect moment, I'm reminded rudely that the world is abrim in assholes."

I took a seat opposite him, a tallish man, steel-grey hair close cropped, high forehead, longish angular face, strong chin, eyes that reflected his Nordic ancestry — a face that beamed out intelligence and humour.

"This meeting—"

"was warranted by the Fates", I interrupted. "Resistance is useless."

"So … apart from ordering some wine and agreeing on pistols at dawn, where do we go from here?"

"I'll start, since you probably need time to cook up something convincing. Hanau is sufficiently close to Frankfurt, it's easily worth a visit, and my conference was something of a bust."

"Well", he began, while tapping a beer map on the table and looking around appreciatively, before returning his gaze to me, "I did warn you about staying out of brassiere design and dandruff sculpture as professions. I knew you'd be no good at either."

It took me a few seconds to work out the "head and shoulders" inference.

"And don't tell me", I interjected brightly, "you're here visiting a maiden auntie."

"Amazing!" he said, shaking his head in wonder. "How you could guess that so quickly!"

The waiter drifted nearby, I ordered two glasses of dry riesling, and we slid into smiles and a handshake.

Vincent Danby, industrial engineer turned patent attorney, had been a friend for more than twenty-five years, ever since early days at university. We had discovered very quickly that we shared a quirky sense of humour, a facility for languages, and an insistent travel itch. My wife, Helena, was joining me in three days, and it didn't surprise me that Marlene was joining Vincent. Our plans had enough overlap that the four of us could spend a day and an evening together, conditional on uxorial approval, of course. Our wives got along well, although when the four of us were together, they became long-suffering because of the antics Vincent and I got up to.

We were sitting at a lovely spot in Hanau Altstadt. Sun came through the broken cloud periodically and warmed the statue of the Brothers Grimm. In fact, we had just spent an absurd half hour remembering all the Grimm fairy tales we could.

"Hindemith was born here too", Vincent pronounced.

"Good for him. Where's his statue?"

Vincent just sipped his wine and gazed at the sky in a display of sublime deafness.

But a few minutes later, Vincent came to life and began talking about the trip he would make to Wertheim in the morning, and wondering if I would like to join him.

"What's in Wertheim?" I asked, knowing full well about its glass museum.

"Well, not the glass museum. I have to dig out some history associated with a group of patent applications I'm working on. And it will also be good for the newsletter."

Vincent produced a newsletter every two months and distributed it to those of his clients and friends he thought would be interested, and it was always exceptionally informative. I was a regular on his mailing list and impressed anew at each issue. He covered history, most often of a particular industry or technology, and he regularly received requests to reproduce his material.

Vincent hesitated here, rubbing an ear lobe in a habit that I recognized, before he spoke again.

"My clients are interested in Wertheim almost exclusively because of its production of laboratory glass and specialist glass items. Of course, there are always a few clients, the normal ones, who are more interested in the history than the technology. I play it up for that sector. But you'd be surprised how many queries and lines of background research arise from the issues of my newsletter."

We talked more about glass. As usual, Vincent was exceptionally well informed on a huge range of topics. I knew enough not to probe too much in an area where he was doing research for a client. It was okay to ask whatever I wanted about any issue of his newsletter that had already been distributed. They would have been vetted carefully to avoid giving away any possible hint about work that a client might have asked him to do.

There was no agenda for the afternoon, so we settled in for a few hours of sun and scenery, and the day would probably also include more wine and perhaps a snack, possibly a shared plate of *Maultaschen*.

Vincent asked me what I was working on at the moment. I gave him a one-minute thumbnail sketch. Vincent nodded. He stared off into the distance and appeared to be trying to decide something.

"Sounds like you're right into things."

This was something of an unlikely comment from Vincent, but I made a sign of acknowledgement and said that I always enjoyed my work.

"Although I have to admit that I find myself doing jobs that increasingly resemble something I've done in the past."

"Is that a problem?" Vincent asked.

"No. Not yet. With luck, not ever."

Vincent just nodded.

"How's your work?" I asked.

There was a long pause, and finally Vincent pulled his gaze away from the sky and looked at me.

"I'm taking early retirement", he announced, in what I thought was a flat tone for something as momentous as this.

I said nothing back to him. I couldn't. I was stunned.

"You're only fifty-six", I said at length.

"Yes … well … the business is changing. I'm liking it less and less. Maybe it's the people or, at least, some of the people. Maybe the work itself is getting to me."

He looked as though he might say something more, but his attention was attracted once more to the clouds.

"When will this happen? What will you do?"

"It's not imminent. The company doesn't know yet."

"What about Marlene?"

Vincent appeared to be scanning the attractive Old Town in Hanau before turning to look at me.

"It's mainly because of Marlene", Vincent said. "Her work is really beginning to get her down. Being a literary agent these days is nothing like what it used to be. The publishing business seems to be going through another major spasm every second month."

All this was news to me, but it didn't surprise me.

"That's where things get interesting", Vincent said, and his expression brightened.

He sipped his wine. I sipped mine. It was a signal that a short hiatus in the conversation had made its appearance.

"She wants to study classical Greek."

This was so unexpected that it was shocking and interesting both at the same time.

"I didn't realize that she was a closet classicist."

Vincent smiled. "Closet classicist! She'll like that."

Another sip of wine, then his glass came down decisively onto the table, and he turned to look at me.

"About a year ago, she handled a novel from a relatively new author, and it was set in ancient and modern Greece. The plot is odd but very inventive and is a reworking in the modern world of Sophocles' play Philoctetes. Marlene had to do a lot of background research — I say 'had to' but it was really a case of 'was driven to' — and, well, she caught the bug."

"Wow!" I said, an unusually adolescent outburst from me.

"That was pretty much my reaction."

"So where…"

"Well, it moved forward from there in stages. Marlene did a large amount of private study on ancient Greek theatre, then took a few courses, and that's when she asked me…"

"Asked you?"

"Yes. If I would mind if she went to Greece to study ancient Greek. I had already been thinking about the next stage in my own life. So I told her about my own need for some kind of change."

Vincent stopped here again, but just looked into the distance.

"Can you tell me what happened next?"

"Oh, sure…" he said, as if coming suddenly out of a trance. "We decided."

Nothing more seemed to be forthcoming. Rather than prod him again, I just waited, looking at Vincent expectantly.

"You probably won't believe this, but we're moving to Crete."

"Crete?" I barked, showing more surprise and astonishment than I intended, but not nearly as much as I felt.

"Yes", Vincent said, displaying the comfort of someone who knows he has made exactly the right decision. "Marlene has found a small private school, and it looks like just the ticket. It's in Heraklion."

By then I had recovered somewhat. "When will all this happen?"

"Oh, not until next summer, at the earliest. And it won't be an immediate bridge-burning exercise. We'll probably try it for a year and then see."

We talked about this venture for almost the next hour, and it was clear that Marlene and Vincent had done a good deal of thinking and planning. There was no doubt in my mind that it would happen.

All this needed reflection. I would be losing regular contact with a very good friend, and that was a matter of some disquiet. I always knew how important Vincent was in my life, but it's true that you don't know what you've got until it threatens not to be there any more.

But a deeper note was sounding somewhere.

What is my own next phase?

I really had no idea.

What did Helena want to do next?

No real idea.

Eighteen months went by quickly. Work was intense and interesting. Marlene and Vincent had indeed wrapped up their careers, staged a party for their best friends, rented their house, and flown off to Crete. Vincent and I were in regular touch. It was abundantly clear that they were both loving what they had embarked upon, no looking back.

Helena and I talked about Marlene and Vincent often. How we missed them. How we were delighted that they had made such a large change with such apparent ease. It was a natural thing then for us to try a pale imitation.

Marlene and Vincent met us in the Heraklion airport after our short flight from Athens. They looked the picture of health and relaxation: nicely bronzed but not burnt, the smiles on their faces leaving no room for stress furrows. In less than an hour, we were at their spacious villa, just fifteen minutes by car or bus from the centre of Heraklion.

We had planned on two weeks, and both Marlene and Vincent had refused point blank even to consider having us stay anywhere but with them. We slid into our accustomed roles of "good friends" in almost less time than it took to reach our first meal together.

The time flew. We did a few of the most essential touristy things, but mostly it was days and evenings spent on their large terrace in the company of food, wine, and friendship.

At the end of the first week, we were embodied firmly in the moment, having lost track of all our previous links to time and space.

The evening was warm and limpid. We had finished an excellent Greek lamb dish, washed down by a superb wine I had never heard of, and held in place by some excellent ouzo.

In bed, we looked at each other. Things had that feeling of the familiar but also the new.

"Well?"

"Yes, well indeed!"

We both smiled and then laughed. We heard what sounded like sympathetic laughter coming from the room next door.

"Is this the new future?" I asked.

"I certainly hope it is", Vincent said, and moved a little closer to me.

CPSIA information can be obtained
at www.ICGtesting.com
Printed in the USA
LVHW111953100519
617444LV00001B/3/P

9 781771 803311